Secrets

Book 11

Marti Talbott's Highlander Series

By

Marti Talbott

-

Editor: *Frankie Sutton*

NOTE: All of Marti Talbott's Books are suitable for young adults 14 and older. Sign up to be notified when new books are published at martitalbott.com

CHAPTER I

In the hills beyond the land of the Haldane, Hendry Buchannan was laird over thousands and he had it all; a fine home, jewels, power over life and death, and the fierceness required to keep his position. Yet nothing mattered more to him than the woman who lie dying in her bed. She gave him five good sons, three of which died in childhood. After the brutal death of his two remaining sons in a war with the MacGraw, she was all the family he had left. Having tried every remedy to save her, he had naught to do but sit beside the bed, hold her hand and watch as she slowly slipped way.

Most considered Hendry Buchannan a handsome man. He kept his light blond hair shoulder length, his matching beard and mustache neatly trimmed, and had striking blue eyes. Arabella, on the other hand, was not the most beautiful woman he had ever seen. There was just something about her that made her irresistible from the very beginning. Perhaps it was her 'come hither' look or the hint of mischief that always seemed to be in her eyes. Whatever it was, he loved her to the depth of his soul and feared he was going to miss her beyond endurance.

The bed she lay in was as large as those found in a king's bedchamber, and Hendry spent a lifetime filling the room with beautiful things for her enjoyment. His was a prosperous clan with more livestock than needed, which allowed him to barter for the finer things in life. Tables, as well as the tops of trunks, displayed golden goblets, silver trays and small, carved boxes filled with jewels. She only wore the jewels when he insisted, and he found her modesty endearing. Now, Laird Buchannan felt he had done right by her and had no regrets on that score. If only he knew how to keep her alive.

Once a tall, vibrant woman with blonde hair, she looked half her normal size, struggled to breathe and opened her blue eyes but a few times during her last hour. When she began to mumble incoherently, he leaned closer, believing her words were meant to be a final goodbye. Instead, she seemed to be reliving a long ago horror he knew nothing about. She spoke of blood everywhere, of believing she was about to die and of doing what had to be done, no matter the cost.

"What, my love, what did you do?"

He would never know if she meant to or not, but Arabella opened her eyes and let an unthinkable secret leave her lips. A mere moment after, she was gone.

Later, Laird Hendry Buchannan could not recall how long he stared at her before he realized she was dead. By the time he became aware, the warmth was gone from the hand he held. Gripped by an inconceivable mixture of rage and grief, he let go of her hand, abruptly stood up and left the bedchamber.

The lavishly decorated great hall in the Buchannan Keep was filled with people awaiting the news, but he ignored them and walked to the table in the center of the room. Not bothering with a goblet, he lifted the pitcher of wine to his lips and drank his fill. When he finished, he wiped the spillage off his mouth and simply said, "She is dead."

Had he glanced at the faces in the room he would have seen more delight than sadness. To most, Arabella was a blight on the land they were glad to finally be shed of. Nevertheless, he did not look at their faces, nor did he care to. Hendry could think of nothing other than her last words. In his mental war between grief and rage, rage was quickly winning.

On the third day, Arabella's burial box was carried to the graveyard. Some women wept appropriately, men looked stoic and knowing of his love for her, everyone assumed Laird Buchannan was too upset to openly grieve. They were wrong. So engrossed was he in his thoughts, the lowering of her box into the ground meant nothing and as soon as it was done, he turned and went home. In a sudden fit of anger, and to everyone's surprise, he gathered her expensive things and threw them out the door. Not one memento of his life with her remained and he vowed never to enter her bedchamber again.

Yet such strong emotions exhausted him and for a full night and late into the next day, he slept. When he awoke, only one name was on his lips - MacGreagor.

*

The midwives who helped bring the triplets, Patrick, Callum and Tavan into the world, were so busy they neglected to mark which was Laird Sawney MacGreagor's eldest son. In all other clans, men fought for the position of laird, but MacGreagors did their own choosing, and normally favored the eldest son of their beloved laird. In this case, the triplets were so much alike in mannerisms, not to mention their dark hair and blue eyes; it would be difficult to choose just one.

Fortunately, Sawney was healthy and they believed they would not be forced to make that decision anytime soon.

The MacGreagor village was not unlike many others. Meandering paths connected the thatched-roof cottages, and the center of their existence was a three-story, stone keep where the laird and his family lived. In front of the Keep was a large courtyard where the evening courting ritual, festivals, weddings and other celebrations took place. A short wall, set in a semicircle, bordered the outside of the courtyard and offered a place to sit, talk and rest. Beyond the courtyard was a long, wide glen with hills on both sides. A practice area had been set aside for the warriors and logs trimmed the other side of the glen, separating it from the graveyard. Farther down, a large corral kept the stallions away from the grazing mares. A nearby loch gave the clan a place to bathe, but the best place for washing clothing and collecting drinking water, was a river that ran behind the village.

The clan shared the work and the food, cared for each other and for the most part, was happy in their relatively peaceful and uncomplicated world. Nevertheless, entertainment was in high demand and their favorite form was gossip.

After two of the triplets, Callum and Patrick, married and began families of their own, the unmarried Tavan became a quiet man, who did not often find himself alone in the great hall of his father's keep. Normally, there were men needing a decision on this issue or that, women coming to see his mother, Mackinzie, or his younger sisters, Bardie and Colina. Yet this evening, his parents were in their bedchamber on the top floor of the three-story building and everyone else was outside.

The great hall was his home and Tavan was comfortable there. New tapestries hung on the walls, a few new weapons, added to the old ones, adorned other walls, and wooden pegs held heavy leather cloaks near the door. His mother's sewing basket sat beside her favorite chair next to the fireplace. His father preferred his seat at the head of the long, polished table in the center of the room and his sisters seemed not to care to sit in that room much at all, except for meals.

Tavan's interest centered on weapons in his youth. He still admired them, and kept himself in good physical condition, just as all the men were required to do. Yet war, even a war with another clan, did not seem likely anytime soon and weapons began to bore him. Now, at twenty-two, he had not taken a wife and did not mind his solitude. If anything, he regretted having so little of it.

He was not yet thirteen when his mother suggested he learn to make wood carvings, just as the man he was named after had. In time, he grew to love the art and became quite good at it. On this day, he decided to carve a goblet similar to the one his mother cherished. Instead of featuring a Gray Wolf on the outside, he favored the image of a Border Collie with long, shaggy hair.

Tavan was seated near the hearth at the far end of the room, hard at work on his new project, when the door opened and a barefoot woman stepped in. She was dressed in the usual sun-bleached white shirt, leather belt, and a somewhat faded green plaid, with a matching measure of the same plaid over her shoulder. He hardly glanced at her before he turned his attention back to his work. "What brings you here this fine day?"

"My shoes are missing."

"Did you look under your bed?" When she did not respond, he finally looked up to see why. The expression on her face told him everything he needed to know - he was a stupid man who just asked a very stupid question. Tavan set his carving down and stood up. "Forgive me; I thought…I mean…where did you last see them?"

"I cleaned them, set them outside to dry and now they are gone. Please tell your father I require a new pair." With that, she turned and went out the door.

"Wait…!" He rushed to catch up, but the door closed before he managed to finish his sentence. "…who are you?" Once more his father was right. He needed to spend less time carving and more time getting to know the names of the people.

Tavan opened the door and stepped out. The courtyard in front of the Keep was nearly empty, no one sat on the short wall, and he could see no barefoot woman walking in the glen. She was not near the stable or the storehouses either. It was possible the woman went around the corner of one of the many cottages, but which one? Tavan sighed and went back to his carving. Whoever she was, she was gone. The incident reinforced his desire *not* to become the clan's next laird. Keeping track of the need for new shoes was the least of a laird's responsibilities.

He highly doubted anyone stole her shoes, for there was little need to steal in a clan that prospered well enough to supply everyone with shoes. Most likely, a puppy found something new to chew on and her shoes would soon be found, although perhaps not in the best condition. Still, as of this moment, she had no shoes and she trusted him to arrange a new pair.

Tavan carefully examined his own shoes. The biggest problem the men had with shoes, once they stopped growing out of them, was the leather straps that laced up to their knees. A way of keeping the straps secured to the shoe seemed to have no solution, other than repeatedly mending them. His straps seemed secure enough, but the woman, whoever she was, had no shoes and he was becoming increasingly bothered by the knowledge. He puffed his cheeks, set his carving on a small table and decided to go look for her.

For the better part of two hours, Tavan walked every crooked path in the constantly growing village, checked near the river, and then walked the full length of the glen. He looked at dozens of female feet, and still did not find the one with no shoes. At length, he decided to take a break from the July heat and find a place to sit under a tree in the forest. Too late, he noticed two sisters sitting on a log not far away. He should not have listened, or at least made his presence known, but he soon found himself fascinated by what they were discussing.

Married to brothers, Logan and Nonie often teased each other about becoming with child, on the same glorious night their husbands came home from helping the MacDuff build more pig pens. The new MacDuff laird seemed to be a clever man, who was eager to learn new ways of making his clan prosper. Therefore, helping the MacDuff was the neighborly thing to do and the men enjoyed their time away. If nothing else, the members of Clan MacDuff could still be counted on for a laugh or two, and several new stories for the men to tell.

In their later stages of pregnancy, Logan and Nonie often walked in the glen together, and rarely made it much farther than the logs near the graveyard, before both were ready to rest a while.

"It will not work," said Logan. She gently rubbed the top of her extended abdomen as she spoke. "Errol always looks at the sex of the child as soon as he can get his hands on it. He hopes the midwife got it wrong, and it is a laddie instead of a lassie each time."

Nonie nodded. "Fib does the same. Suppose we both have lassies or laddies this time? What do we do then?"

Logan giggled. "Twould be just our luck. You have three laddies and I have four lassies, surely God will grant us the reverse this time. I care not to see the disappointment in either of our husband's faces, and Errol so wants a son."

"I know, 'tis why we intend to give him one. But how, sister, how do we switch the babes without anyone knowing?"

"There is but one way, we must give birth at the same time and in the same cottage."

Nonie wrinkled her brow. "Would the midwife agree to keep our secret, do you think?"

"Aye, she will agree. I know something I should not know about her."

"Oh, do tell."

"Nay, I promised not to," said Logan. "Nevertheless, I am willing to break that promise if need be."

"What if our labor does not begin at the same time?"

"That would be just our luck too. I suppose when the pains start for the first, the other must mount a horse and ride until the water breaks."

Nonie rolled her eyes. "Have you tried getting on a horse in your ninth month? We would need a ladder and the horse would surely object."

"What then?"

"I do not know. Perhaps…"

There was no mistaking Sawney's whistle. Although it did not signal danger, it was his way of telling the people to gather. Tavan waited until the women slowly got up and started for the courtyard, before he stood and followed. He would have liked hearing the rest of their plan, but that was not to be.

Now he had two problems. He could not find the shoeless woman, and he could not decide if he should tell someone what Logan and Nonie were up to. He understood Errol's need to father a son; it was what all men wanted, yet no matter their good intentions, the sisters were treading on forbidden ground. He could already think of two things that could go wrong.

Tavan crossed the glen and made his way through the people to stand beside his brothers. "What is it?" he asked.

"I do not know," Patrick answered.

Sawney held up his hand to silence everyone. "I have counted the days of no rain and they number forty-three. The stream that runs through the pasture has nearly dried up and the farmers need our help. Tomorrow, the hunters will not hunt. Instead, they will help water the gardens and herd the livestock over the hill to the loch. This must be done twice a day. Every lad who is able must help keep the crops alive. There is no way to know how long it will be before the rain returns. Are you willing?"

"Aye," the clansmen all said at once.

"Lasses, keep close watch over the children. When there is little water, the wild beasts come down out of the hills. See that you are well armed and that the children are within your sight. Do you agree?"

"Aye," said all the women.

"Very well, sleep well tonight. The work ahead will be long and hard."

The evening meal in Laird MacGreagor's great hall was normally a lively affair, considering the family now consisted of eight adults and four children, although at twelve, Bardie resented still being considered a child. Sawney and Mackinzie's eldest daughter, Colina, was fast turning into a sought after young woman.

Now that they were older and everyone knew how to tell them apart anyway, the triplets wore their dark hair and mustaches in different styles. Patrick and Graw gave Laird MacGreagor his first grandson, while Kylie presented her husband, Callum, with both a boy and a girl. Their seating arrangements in the tall back chairs around the table were by design, so at least one adult was next to each child. A rotating group of assigned women prepared meals in the kitchen and considered it an honor to serve their Laird and his family. It was also a good way for the serving women to eavesdrop whenever possible, and perhaps have something exciting to tell the clan.

"Tavan," Sawney said as they began to eat. "You will move your things into the Carley cottage for now."

"You wish me out of your sight, Father?" Tavan asked.

"'Tis because he snores too loud," Bardie whispered to Colina.

Tavan playfully glared across the table at his little sister. "I heard that."

"Your mother and I will take up residence in your bedchamber, so the lads can go to the widows on the top floor and watch for fires. The leaves of the Aspen are turning gray and the undergrowth is dry in the forest."

"I fear nothing as much as a forest fire." Mackinzie muttered, more to herself than the family. Her shade of hair was more auburn than brown, and both her daughters had inherited it, although only Colina had Mackinzie's green eyes. "If even one lad is not careful he can kill many."

"True," Sawney agreed. "And when the rains come, we must expect lightning."

It was easy to tell when something excited Bardie and she could hardly wait for a break in the conversation. "Did you see them?" she asked.

"See what?" all three triplets asked at the exact same moment.

"Five reindeer at the far end of the loch. I have never before seen reindeer."

"Reindeer, are you certain?" asked Sawney.

"Well no, but they have very long horns that stick straight up instead of out, their fur is white in the front, and they are much larger than our skinny little red deer."

Callum frowned. "It has begun much sooner than we expected. The wildcats, the bears and the wolves will not be far behind."

Sawney nodded. "They will not like it, but the lads best guard the lasses while they bathe from now on."

Patrick chucked, "Mother will protect them."

Mackinzie rolled her eyes. "I have already fought a wildcat and a wolf, neither of which I care to fight again. This time I shall run…and much faster than you think I can."

Sawney smiled at his wife. "Please do. You are very brave, but I do not intend to let anything hurt you ever again." He took another bite, chewed and swallowed before he asked, "Callum, you went with the hunters today, is there no word of how the other clans are doing?"

Callum was about to take a bite, put his spoon down instead and folded his arms. "I planned to leave this for later, but there is a bit of news. First, the MacDuff laird has declared that any man who does not work shall be banished."

"Good heavens," Patrick said, "he will lose half his clan."

Callum shook his head. "Nay, they fear being banished more than working. 'Tis a good move on his part."

"I agree," said Sawney. "The MacDuff will learn to take pride in their work, just as our laddies do. 'Tis a good move indeed. Is there more news to be had?"

Callum turned his gaze downward. "Two Swintons are dead and it is thought they were attacked by the English."

Sawney immediately stopped eating. "Why do they think that?"

"The bodies were discovered in the far south of their land. Who else could have done it? The Swintons are not at war with any other clan."

"Aye," said Sawney, "but there are many reasons to kill a lad. Perhaps they tried to take a horse, or even a lass. Perhaps they saw something other lads did not want them to see, or…"

"Or, it might have been the English, hoping to start a war," said

Patrick.

Mackinzie suddenly lost her appetite. "I pray you are wrong."

"As do we all, Mother," said Callum, "but it will happen someday. They fear us, they lust after our land and they want us to pay their taxes. 'Tis enough we must give tithe to the church and support our own king."

"If only there was some way to confound the English king," said Colina. At nearly seventeen, she had yet to find the right husband, although she had walked with several men during their nightly courting ritual. Some were boring, some arrogant and some she found completely stupid. There was a man for her; she just had not walked with him yet.

Patrick grinned at Colina. "I have it; we shall send *you* to him. We shall give you a good scrubbing, put flowers in your hair and make him worry what the Scots are up to."

If Colina could have reached that far, she would have hit him. Instead, she gave him her sternest look. "Have I mentioned how unsightly you are, Patrick?"

"I am cut to the bone," said Callum.

"As am I," Tavan added.

It was definitely time to change the subject and she had just the thing. "Father," Colina began, "Why do we call it the Carley Cottage?"

Sawney finished chewing his last bite and pushed his bowl away. "You do not know? Perhaps you should stay to listen to the stories instead of running off with your friends of an evening. Carley was my aunt and a very special lass at that. It was she who helped win the war with the Davidsons."

Finished with his meal, Patrick leaned back in his chair and took hold of Graw's hand. "I feel a story coming on. Have you heard this one, my love?"

"Once or twice, I believe," she answered, returning her husband's grin.

"In that case," Sawney said, "I shall save it for later. I am far more interested in why Tavan has not yet taken a wife. Son, do you intend to remain unmarried much longer?"

The room quieted and all eyes were on Tavan, who took a deep breath and tried to think of an answer he had not already given on previous nights. "Father, you do not hope I will marry just anyone, do you?"

"Of course not, I wish you to be in love when you marry. Perhaps I can help."

"I do not require your help."

Sawney studied his son's eyes. "You have already chosen."

"Perhaps."

"And perhaps not," Mackinzie said.

"True," said Tavan.

"Wife, I believe your son *has* chosen. Now all we must do is see the lass falls in love with him."

"You wish to make her fall in love with me?" Tavan asked. "I have believed you capable of many things, Father, but that is not one of them."

"You know what I mean. If you tell me who she is, I might manage to…"

"To what, interfere? The last time you interfered, both the lad and the lass stayed clear of you for months," said Tavan.

Sawney wrinkled his brow and looked at his wife. "Is that true?"

Mackinzie tried hard to hide her smile. "The fault is mine, I neglected to warn you of her great dislike for the lad."

Callum wrinkled his brow. "Did they not marry anyway?"

"Aye," said Colina. "Together, they conspired to avoid Father and fell in love in spite of him."

"There you see, it was I who brought them together after all."

Tavan waited until they finished laughing before he said, "I will gladly sleep in the Carley cottage. Perhaps then I can spend more time on my carving."

Sawney took his wife's hand. "Do you see how your son tries to change the subject?"

"He is *my* son, is he?" Mackinzie asked.

"Aye, he is your only unmarried son, for which there seems no remedy."

Tavan finished his last bite, washed it down with a swallow of wine and stood up. "The only way to avoid your endless questions on this subject is to take my carving outside." With that, he walked to the small table, retrieved his block of wood and went out the door.

CHAPTER II

Laird Buchannan sat alone in his great hall, having sent everyone away, including his second and third in command. The needs of his clan were many, and their worry over the lack of rain kept his mind somewhat occupied during the day, but what Arabella told him was never far from his thoughts. He had a decision to make and he alone could make it.

Hendry was a young man who had a lust for all things new and different, when he became laird of the Buchannans. He was wise in the ways of clan warfare, but not so wise when it came to women. Arabella captured his heart without even trying. She wore MacGreagor colors, and had a way of appearing, and then disappearing back into the forest. Several times he tried to find her and once, when he could not, he heard her laughter echo through the trees.

It served to make him that much more determined. He would have her, he vowed, and no man could stop him. It took two more tries to catch her and when he grabbed her from behind, she turned, put her arms around his neck and kissed him with a passion he did not believe possible. At least, that is how he remembered it. He knew then, having her once would never be enough.

There was a problem, but a man with such a burning desire could, and would find a way around any stumbling block. Yet, there was some measure of guilt to be had as well, and for that reason, he stayed clear of the MacGreagors after they were married. The weeks became months, the months turned into years, and if anyone thought it was strange that neither the MacGreagors nor the Buchannans sought each other out, they did not mention it to him. Everyone knew why, he supposed and it was simply none of their business. Not once did he consider righting the wrong he had done, for Arabella was life to him.

Laird Buchannan paced the length of the great hall for the better part of an hour before he was certain he had no choice. To get what he wanted, he had to face his past head on. It was decided then -- he would go to the MacGreagor village just as soon as the rain returned.

In the middle of the glen, Sharla MacGreagor stood with her hands on her hips glaring at the young woman she thought of as her best friend. "The fault is yours."

Jenae's mouth dropped. She watched a third young woman hurry down a path between the cottages and disappear. "Mine? How am I to blame?" No two women could have been less alike than these two. Sharla was tall, with wavy, dark blonde hair she wore in a tight braid, while the much shorter Jenae preferred her lighter hair loosely braided and piled on top of her head, especially when it was hot. About the only thing they had in common was their blue eyes, although Jenae's were a lighter shade.

"It was you who first noticed Parlan looking at me."

"Aye, but I did not tell you to say it to Senga. Look what you have done. She fancies him and you made her run off in tears."

"I only said I thought he preferred me and not her."

"Nay, you did not say that at all. You said he preferred you, not that *you thought* he did. You are very cruel when you want to be, Sharla."

"You are mistaken, I said *I thought.* I remember it clearly."

"I remember it just as clearly and you did not."

"'Tis your fault anyway. You should not have told me you saw Parlan watching me. I would never have noticed him otherwise."

"I give up; nothing is ever your fault." Jenae turned and walked away. It was too hot in the afternoon sun anyway, and the shade of the trees at the edge of the forest looked very inviting.

Sharla was furious and headed across the glen in the opposite direction. How dare Jenae talk to her that way? She had half a mind never to call her friend again. Of course she did things wrong, and just as often as anyone else. She was exceedingly honest and more than willing to admit it when the fault was truly hers. This time, it simply was not.

She was about to go to her cottage when she spotted Tavan coming out of the Keep. She liked Tavan as well as any man, she supposed. One thing was for certain, if she married Tavan and he became laird, no one would talk to her the way Jenae just did. She would be honored, respected and never accused of lying...if she were mistress of the MacGreagors.

The more she thought about it, the more she liked the idea, and when Tavan sat down on the short wall in the courtyard, she decided to go see what he was up to. By the time she arrived, he seemed so intent on his carving, she decided not to disturb him. Just then, he looked up and noticed her.

Tavan didn't mean to, but he puffed his cheeks. He didn't know this one's name either. "Have you come for the courting," he asked without realizing what he was implying.

She was surprised by his question and decided she should be a little harder to get than that. "Not particularly. I have often seen you carve, but never up close. Is it hard?"

"It was at first. It takes hours of practice to get the knife to go where you want it to. Have you tried it?" When she giggled, he finally looked up again. She was as pleasing as any other lass and her laughter was soft and easy on the ears.

"I would probably cut myself."

"You would not be the first. I have several carving battle scars on my fingers."

"What is the best kind of wood?"

Before he could answer, Mackinzie came out, walked to him and leaned against the wall on the other side of Tavan. "Sharla, you are looking well."

"Thank you, I am very well."

That was her name, Sharla, Tavan thought. Nevertheless, he was far more interested in what his mother was up to, than he was in teaching Sharla how to carve. "Has Father sent you to plague me with more questions?"

"Aye," Mackinzie answered, "He only wants you to be happy. I wish the same, but I am happiest when your father has a mystery to solve. Just now, learning your secret is the most intriguing mystery I have heard in ages. Can you not give me just a hint?"

"Perhaps there is no mystery."

"And perhaps there is?"

Tavan smiled, "You know me too well, Mother. Outwitting you is never easily done."

Mackinzie put her hand on her son's shoulder. "Outwitting you is never easy either. Allow me something to tell him."

He looked down and thought about it for a moment. "Tell him, the lass I love most in the world is in need of new shoes."

Mackinzie was delighted with his answer, quickly made her excuse and went back inside.

Sharla was a bit disappointed. She couldn't help but look down and her shoes were perfectly fine. "You have chosen a wife?"

"Nay, but my father hopes I have. You will not tell him, will you?"

She brightened right up. "What will you give me to keep your secret?"

He stopped carving and looked at her playful eyes. "What do you require?"

"Well, I would like a castle on a hill, a pure white horse and…"

"A castle on a hill? Which hill?"

She slowly uncurled her first finger and pointed west. "That one. 'Tis the highest and from there I can see everything."

"Good choice, I shall begin the building immediately." When he finally smiled, so did she.

*

Inside the Keep, Sawney rolled his eyes, "That is no help at all. The lass Tavan loves most in the world is you."

Nearly every member of the family tried to get a look at Mackinzie's shoes and discovered they were indeed beginning to wear out. She took her seat next to Sawney and frowned. "Husband, Tavan has little choice here. It is nearly time for our harvest festival. Perhaps we should invite other clans to join us this year."

"We invite other clans every year."

"Aye, we invite the lairds and their families, but we do not invite the people. I say it is time to give Tavan more lasses to choose from."

"She is right father," said Patrick. "Send Tavan to invite them."

"You doubt he has chosen a lass here?" asked Sawney.

"Father," said Callum, "we would know if he fancied one here. Being smitten is not easy to hide. You said yourself, a lad always knows where the lass he loves is, and Tavan looks for no one in particular."

"Until today," Colina put in. When she looked up, everyone was staring at her. "Well, he has been outside for hours, which you must admit is very odd. I saw him hide beside a cottage listening to two lasses talk. When has he ever done that?"

"Who was he listening…?"

"I saw him too, hiding behind a tree near the graveyard," said Graw.

Mackinzie gleefully clasped her hands together, "He looks for someone, I am certain of it."

"Does he hope to watch her without her knowing?" asked Kylie. "Why does he not just approach her?"

It was a question no one had the answer to. Patrick exchanged glances with Callum and nodded. "He is never shy, but a lass might make him so. Do you agree?"

"Perhaps," said Callum.

"Well I feel sorry for him," said Bardie. "Now all of you will be watching everything he does. Mother and Father will pretend to go to their bedchamber to talk and instead, they will peek out every window. The rest of you will find a reason to go to the second floor to do the same, or outside to watch him from afar. He'll not have a moment's peace and he will certainly not approach her if we are all watching."

"She is right," said Sawney. "I forbid anyone to watch him."

Patrick laughed, "And who will forbid you? You are the worst of us."

Sawney lifted his chin in defiance. "A laird must have some privileges."

"And his wife," Mackinzie added.

Graw giggled, "And his daughters, his sons and their wives."

Sawney rolled his eyes. "I relent."

*

Sharla managed to seat herself on the short wall not far from Tavan so she could watch him carve, but she soon lost interest and looked at the young women beginning to gather in the courtyard instead. "Your sister will marry soon."

"Will she? Which fine lad will she marry?" Tavan asked.

"Oh I do not know just yet, but I will soon enough. I watch that sort of thing carefully."

"Why?"

"Because I like guessing and I am rarely wrong. There are two she fancies, and…"

"Two, I am surprised. To hear Colina tell it, she does not approve of any of them."

"She is too particular. All lasses must settle for one fault or another."

Tavan found himself captivated by her opinion. "Must a lad settle as well?"

She tried to look as serious as she could. "Lads are such contrary beings, it is hard to say why they fancy one lass over another. I believe it has to do with the moon."

He was even more intrigued. "What does the moon have to do with it?"

"Well, when the moon is shining, a lad is like a beloved dog waiting to be petted, but when it is dark, he is like a gray wolf, sneaking through the trees searching for his prey."

Tavan stared into her eyes for a moment more than he should have, and it wasn't until she began to smile that he realized she was teasing. "Do you trick lads often?"

"No more often than I can. I must go now. Do not forget to build my castle." She scooted down off the wall and walked away.

*

No one believed the drought would last long - it never had before. Frequent rain was a way of life in Scotland and there was nothing unusual that spring to give them any warning. In mid-July, the grass in the MacGreagor glen began to turn brown, but even that was not uncommon. Nevertheless, the people watched the skies much more often than before, hoping a gentle breeze meant they would soon see clouds on the horizon.

As the clan grew, so did the need for more farm land as well as wood for building. Clearing the land around a smaller adjoining glen seemed the perfect answer, especially since a shallow creek flowed down the center of it. It was normally more than enough to water both the land and the livestock, and never had anyone seen it dry up. Now that it had, no member of the MacGreagor village remained idle.

Stored grain from the previous year provided enough bread, but baking bread and churning milk into cream, butter and cheese, was grueling for the women in such heat. It was up to the men to see to watering the crops and it was strenuous work, especially since there was a wooded hill between the pasture and the loch. Each morning the men spread out, and it was not unusual for Sawney's triplet sons to stand side by side on the path, handing full buckets of water up one side of the hill and down the other. As well, they passed empty ones in the opposite direction.

To keep the sun from burning their light skin any more than it already had, the men were rotated into the shade of the trees, where the work was cooler and they could take off their shirts. Spilled water made the path slick and it was on one such rotation that Tavan slipped and fell to his knees.

Exhausted, he slumped down, hung his head and closed his weary eyes. The hottest part of the day was upon them, sweat constantly ran down his chest, and soaked into his belt and kilt. Even the band around his hair could not keep the sweat out of his eyes. What he wanted most in the world was to jump in the loch, clothes and all, and cool off. Unfortunately, that delight would have to wait another hour or two.

He had not been there long before he opened his eyes to find a woman standing right in front of him. He was looking to see if she was the one with no shoes when she knelt down. She dipped her cloth in his bucket of water, put her hand under his chin and lifted his face. As gently as she could, she blotted his forehead and then the rest of his face with her cool cloth. He could not help but close his eyes again and draw in the luxury of her kind and caring touch. A second time, she soaked the cloth in the water and blotted his face, careful not to rub his sunburn.

When he, at last, looked up, her blue eyes held the same sparkle he had often seen in his mother's eyes, and it made him smile. Before he could thank her, she stood up and went back into the forest.

Just coming over the top of the hill, Patrick noticed her and then frowned. "Have I given you permission to rest?" He held out his hand and helped his brother up.

Tavan ignored him. "Who was that?"

"You do not know?"

"I do not recall seeing that one before."

"Father is right, you need to set aside your carving and meet the clan. You may be their laird someday, you know."

Callum finally caught up, looked at the mud on his brother's knees and rolled his eyes. "Have I given you permission to...?"

"Brother, Tavan has met Kristin and knows not who she is."

"Impossible," said Callum, "every unmarried lad in the world dreams of Kristin."

Tavan picked up the bucket of water and handed it to Patrick. "We are holding up the line, brothers." Once more, the triplets spread out and went back to silently passing the buckets. Not long after, they heard a man shout something in the glen and paused to listen.

"I have a son!" the shout came again.

"'Tis Errol," said Patrick. "After four daughters, at last, his wife has given him a son."

Tavan passed the next bucket on. The triplets didn't keep secrets from each other, at least Tavan didn't think they did, and he was tempted to share what he heard the pregnant sisters discussing. Still, he did not know if they had given birth at the same time. If so, was the other baby a girl or a boy? No, he could wait until he had the answer to that question before deciding what to do. Errol was a good man who deserved a son -- even if it was not truly his.

*

"At least the days are getting shorter," Tavan said, sitting down between Callum and Patrick in the courtyard, He leaned back against the cool rocks of the short wall and heaved a sigh of relief. The best shade the village had to offer now that the sun was going down, was in front of the three-story keep the triplets were born in.

"It will rain tomorrow," Patrick said.

Callum looked up at the clear blue sky. "You say that every day."

"Aye and the chances of being right increase every day." Patrick leaned forward and looked around Tavan at Callum, "Shall we tell him about Kristin?"

"Tell him what?" Callum asked.

"They say Kristin is but a whisper in the wind, a wisp of smoke and the song in the trees."

Tavan shrugged. "She looked real enough to me."

"The sun has made him daft," said Callum.

"Aye," Patrick agreed. "Many a lass sings in the forest, but not like this one. Kristin has the voice of twenty angels."

Tavan used his cloth to wipe the last of the sweat off his forehead. "You are the daft ones, but I forgive you. Tell me where she lives and I shall ask her to sing for us."

Callum shook his head. "No one knows where she lives. She appears and then disappears into the forest. The last time I saw her, she was walking out of the morning mist, pretty as you please."

"She wears MacGreagor colors. Someone must know where she lives," said Tavan.

Patrick shrugged. "Callum speaks the truth. Several have searched and none have found her."

"How then do you know her name?" Tavan waited, but neither of his brothers had an answer, so he slowly and painfully got to his feet. "Well, the next time she walks out of the mist, ask her to come to the Keep and sing for us. All I intend to do is eat and go to bed."

*

Sleep came easily to the hard working MacGreagor clan; all except the night guards and Tavan. He still did not know which woman asked for new shoes, but decided to dismiss that worry. After all this time, she must have talked to Sawney and gotten a new pair…that is if she didn't find the old one. He let the woman down and it bothered him, but there was little he could do about it.

During the evening meal, his mother announced that the sisters had indeed given birth in the same cottage, at the same time. They presented each husband with the sex of the child he longed for, and both women survived the birth. Errol had his son and at long last, Fib had a daughter.

Tavan considered saying something then, but it seemed too late to bring it up. Besides, he couldn't be certain the sisters truly had deceived their husbands by switching babies.

It was the fair-haired Kristin who kept him awake the longest. Never had he imagined such a tender moment with a woman. When he closed his eyes, he could still feel her fingertips under his chin and her cool cloth against his face. Yet it was her blue eyes he remembered most. One moment they were kind and the next, mischievous. He couldn't help but wonder if she washed the faces of other men, or just his. Before he could ponder the question further, he fell asleep.

*

To the delight of everyone, morning brought dark clouds and nearly the whole clan gathered outside, hoping to feel the first rain drops. A sprinkle brought a shout, and then another and another until the sprinkles became a downpour, forcing everyone to happily run for cover. Sawney declared a day of rest and no one needed it more than he. Still, the men liked to gather in the great hall, share a word or two with their laird and pass the time. What else was there to do, except annoy their wives in small cottages? There was not a man among them who did not have a face burned by the sun.

Long ago, Sawney made Tavan his first in command, but his son cared more for his carving than the inner workings of the clan. Still, Tavan listened and when Sawney questioned him, Tavan had most of the answers right. Tavan carried out each assignment without complaint, and did it well; he just hadn't taken much of an interest in the people.

As all lairds knew, it was important to surround himself with young men, quick on their feet with sharp eyesight and minds. It did not hurt if the young men were unmarried and unaccustomed to worrying about a wife and children, but Sawney always knew when one became distracted by thoughts of a woman he fancied. On this morning, Tavan had all the symptoms.

The first sign was Tavan's sudden disinterest in his carving. Secondly, he was impatient to be assigned a duty, even though it was to be a day of rest. Elated, Sawney decided to send his son to see if the rain was watering the farmlands sufficiently. Of course it was, but if Tavan guessed it was a trumped up duty, he didn't let on. He simply nodded, grabbed a cloak off a wooden peg near the door and left.

A slow smile crossed Sawney's face as he glanced at his other two sons. "Do you let him ride alone?"

Just as pleased, Callum and Patrick hurried to catch up with their brother. Halfway down the path to the corral, Patrick slapped Callum on the back. "'Tis Kristin."

"Aye, 'tis Kristin. Did I not say it would work?"

"He will have our heads when he discovers what we have done."

"He will thank us someday, mark my words." The closer they got to Tavan, the softer Callum talked. "I like her very much. She will make him a good wife."

"I like her too."

Tavan did not want company just now, but as second in command, he expected it. There was little danger of being attacked, but one could not be too careful. The capture and ransom of a second in command put the entire clan in jeopardy. Just the same, looking for Kristin with them tagging along would be far more difficult. There were plenty of excuses he could use to go into the forest where he last saw her, but with his brothers waiting, he could not stay long enough to actually search for her.

The path into the adjoining glen was wet and to prevent the horses from slipping, especially where the path was not exactly level, the triplets kept a slow pace. Despite the rain, farmers still went about their business tending the hen houses and pig pens. A fence, separating the pasture from the gardens was in need of repair, and it was a full time job for two young men in leather cloaks, to keep the cows out of the tempting gardens. It was clearly time to build stonewalls to replace the wooden ones, but that work would have to wait for winter.

Some of the vegetables were harvested early and the seeds dried for planting the next year. Several types of fruits and vegetables grew wild, but they needed herbs and spices to make them palatable. Celery herb, fennel and chives could make most anything taste better, and honey sweetened orange cloudberry juice was a favorite among the children. Yet bread, they were convinced, kept them alive and normally, they bartered cattle with other clans for barley and oats. However, this year they might be forced to buy what they needed from places as far away as Ireland or France.

The cattle were first to graze the meadow and the sheep got what was left, but with little rain; the grass was just beginning to revitalize. It would be a while before either could enjoy a full day of grazing. For that reason, many of the cows were still in the forest gleaning what they could. On a far off hillside, collies were busy obeying the whistles of the sheepherder. Other dogs, needed to alert the farmers of danger, stayed out of the rain as best they could, but nothing kept the chickens from pecking seeds off the ground.

The vegetables would soon need to be harvested, those the sun had not burned, that is. White carrots, onions and turnips grew beneath the earth, and only their leaves were damaged, but other vegetables such as cabbage and peas were not so fortunate. Still, the rain would help save what was left, and as the triplets rode the path at the edge of the glen, the plants and the leaves of the fruit trees, seemed to be reviving right before their eyes. The wild cherries were already harvested, but the wild pears wouldn't be ready for another month or so.

Tavan needn't have worried about finding Kristin. Once they passed the fruit trees, he spotted her standing at the edge of the forest watching them. The sprawling branches and abundant leaves of the tree she stood under appeared to be keeping her dry enough. Now, all he needed was a reason to go talk to her.

"Kristin!" Patrick shouted. He turned his horse, headed that direction and as he hoped, both Callum and Tavan followed. As soon as he reached her, Patrick swung down and joined her under the tree. "Shall I take you home?"

That twinkle was in her eyes again when she briefly glanced up at Tavan. "Nay, with four brothers and six sisters, all younger, I prefer the solitude of the forest."

Just as his brother had, Callum dismounted and walked to her. "I can see why."

Tavan felt a little self-conscience, now that he was the only one still mounted, so he slid down and joined his brothers. He wanted to thank her for washing his face the day before, but not with his brothers there. Suddenly, he remembered her. "You have new shoes, I see."

She put her hands on her hips and glared at him, "Nay, I found the old ones."

There was no mistaking the sarcasm in her voice, so he returned her glare, "Were they under your bed?"

"If they were, I would not confess it." Clearly annoyed, she folded her arms. "When I told your father I would not need new ones, he had not heard. Did you not tell him?"

"I did not tell him, because you did not tell me your name."

Patrick and Callum exchanged knowing glances. It was indeed Kristin Tavan fancied, for he was so engrossed in his conversation with her, he had no idea either of his brothers were still there.

"You do not know my name?" Kristin shot back. "We grew up in the same clan and you do not..."

Patrick rolled his eyes, "He carves."

"I know," said Kristin, not taking her glare off of Tavan. "I have seen his carvings."

"And?" asked Tavan.

"And what?"

"Do they please you?"

"One or two."

"Only one or two? How many of my carvings..."

"Brother," Callum interrupted. "We are to see if the rain has watered the gardens sufficiently, remember?"

"I remember." At last, he lowered his eyes and looked away. It was not at all the kind of exchange he hoped to have with her, and he hated to leave on such a sour note. "I am happy you found your shoes."

"Not as happy as I am," said Kristin.

Tavan wanted to calm the situation, but Callum kept pulling on his belt, making him back away. "We would be honored to take you home."

"Nay, I prefer it here."

He nodded, finally turned around and mounted his horse. He tried not to, but as he rode away, he looked back. Kristin was gone.

"Still, she does not say where she lives," Patrick said, as they continued down the glen, each nodding to acknowledge the various farmers.

"She is Samuel's daughter," said Tavan, "and she has no brothers and sisters."

"And you know this...how?" Callum asked.

"I asked Mother, once she promised not to tell Father."

Patrick chuckled. "Mother never keeps a secret from Father."

"She will keep this one. I promised to keep her secret in return."

"What secret?" both of Tavan's brothers asked at the same time. He only smiled and rode on ahead.

At the end of the glen, the farmers and their families, including Samuel and his daughter, lived in a small village of their own. They were a close knit group, who also served as guards and the first line of defense should invaders come. There was not much danger of that, since the nearest neighbor in that direction was the MacDuff, and the MacDuff were more practiced at surrendering than fighting.

Also outside in the pouring rain, Samuel happily watched the small stream in the middle of the glen fill with water. As the eldest of the farmers, he was respected and often looked to for advice, which he found flattering. His hair was such a light blond, one could hardly notice the gray in it. Yet there was no hope of hiding the coming of age in his somewhat darker beard and mustache.

There was something missing in his life, but he tried not to think about it too often. He had Kristin to care for and it was enough - it had to be. Yet he often watched the edges of the forest just in case. It was an old habit he never could quite break, no matter how hard he tried.

When he saw the triplets coming, he waved them over. Then he rested an arm on top of his shovel handle, and waited until they were near enough to hear him. "Tell Sawney three calves lost to one beast or another, I cannot tell which. Wolves perhaps or even a bear. We heard wolves howling in the night. If the rain stops, I mean to build a fire or two to keep them away."

"I will tell him," said Tavan. "Have you any news of the other clans?"

"Nay, not today," Samuel answered.

Tavan nodded. He wanted to stay longer, but he could not think of a reason to. "Send word if you need lads to help you."

"I will," Samuel said. He watched the three ride back the way they came, and as always, searched the edge of the forest with his eyes. When he spotted Kristin watching the triplets, he smiled. She had asked questions about Tavan the week before and Samuel hoped she favored him. If he had to lose her, as all fathers must, he could not think of a better man to give her to.

When he took his daughter to the village of an evening, as he often did, Kristin never joined the other unmarried women in the courtyard. She only stood in the forest and watched. Tavan did not ask a woman to walk with him either, and Samuel wondered if they waited for each other without knowing it. The thought made him smile. Love certainly had strange ways.

CHAPTER III

Sawney could not believe it. He questioned everyone while the triplets were gone and no one knew which woman caught Tavan's eye. He asked his daughters, his closest friends and advisors, both his daughter-in-laws, and still he had no hint of her identity. The only one he did not ask was Mackinzie, but he needn't bother; his wife never kept secrets from him.

At the evening meal, Tavan reported the lost calves and warned Sawney not to be alarmed if Samuel started fires to keep them away. The thought of wolves so close to Kristin's home bothered Tavan, but he did not bring it up. He was worried about the other farmers too, he reminded himself.

Soon, his family turned to discussing other things and he went back to being his old, quiet self, only now he had Kristin to think about. She was annoyed with him and she had a right to be. Still, she came to report her missing shoes before she so gently washed his face and she was not upset then. It made no sense at all. He was reminded how little he knew of women, at least women outside his immediate family. His mother and sister had a look about them that warned of trouble, and perhaps all women did. Yet Kristin seemed happy enough to see his brothers.

"Tavan?"

He suddenly looked up. "Aye, Father."

"You do not hear me. Is it because you think of a bonnie lass instead?"

Tavan puffed his cheeks. "Father, have you no other entertainment? Perhaps you might tell a story, or better yet, have you asked your eldest daughter why she has not yet married?" He ignored his sister's glare, excused himself and went outside.

Sawney watched him go, and then looked at the table near the hearth. "He has left his carving."

"Perhaps he has given it up," Mackinzie said.

"He will take it up again once he is married. Tell me; is the Carley cottage suitable for a family?" Sawney asked.

"My love," said Mackinzie, "You have him married already? Can he not court her first?"

Sawney raised an eyebrow. "Is that where he goes? The courtyard? This I must see."

Bardie folded her arms. "I thought we agreed not to watch him."

Sawney took a deep breath and let it out. "So we did."

Patrick grinned at his littlest sister, "Quick, guard the stairs so he cannot go up and peek out the window."

"I am but a child, how can I stop him?"

"She is right," said Graw. "I will help her."

"And so will I," Kylie added.

Sawney stared for a moment at each of his sons. "Are you not going to help me? Have you no regulation over your wives?"

At the same exact time and in the same exact way, the brothers said, "Nay."

*

The sunshine was back, but at least a good downpour watered the land and the gardens well enough for a day or two. After the morning meal, Tavan announced he was off to find more wood suitable for carving. The men were already beginning to gather in the great hall and when Sawney did not object, Tavan left.

If he did not know better, Tavan would think Sharla was waiting for him. He dismissed that thought, crossed the courtyard and walked right past her into the glen. If Kristin truly had the voice of twenty angels, perhaps he could find her just by listening. On the other hand, she was a farmer's daughter and this early in the morning, she was probably milking cows. He could think of nothing but Kristin, and was wondering what kind of madness had begun to possess him, when he heard a voice behind him.

"Do you ignore me, Tavan MacGreagor?" Sharla asked, practically running to catch up with him.

"Forgive me, I did not mean to." He stopped and turned to her. "Have you a need?"

His question caught her a little off guard. She meant to mention the castle he promised to build for her, but just now his voice sounded cold and distant. "A need? Let me see, what need could I possibly have?" She laid a forefinger on the side of her face and thought for a moment. "I remember now, I was wondering when we are to celebrate the harvest." It was a stupid question and she knew it, but it was the only one she could think of.

"Perhaps you might ask Mother." He glanced toward the courtyard, spotted Colina and nodded that direction. "My sister might know."

"You do not care about such things?"

"I care, but first we must bring in the harvest. I suspect it is too soon to plan the feast."

"Of course it is, forgive my foolishness. Yesterday, you asked which lads mean to have your sister and I neglected to answer. Shall I answer now?"

"Please," he said, just to be polite. Tavan once more glanced at Colina, who seemed content just to talk to her friends. No doubt she was telling them what Samuel said about the wolves. Samuel reminded him of Kristin, but Sharla was the woman standing in front of him and he could not just walk away.

"They are Parlan and Alec."

"Parlan? Does he not prefer Senga?"

"Well, if he does, he should not be watching your sister."

"Merely looking at a lass does not mean he is smitten," Tavan was tired of this discussion already and began to slowly walk on.

Again, Sharla hurried to catch up. "Parlan is a good lad. Perhaps he does not prefer either of them. I guess I could be wrong."

"Yesterday you said you were rarely wrong."

"I rarely am. I could be wrong about being wrong, you know." At last, it made him smile and she was relieved. It occurred to her she should leave well enough alone. "I must go, but before I do, do you care to place a wager on which your sister marries?"

He stopped and turned to her. "I like a wager as well as any lad, but with my sister it could be years before I can collect."

"Well, if you change your mind, come find me." Sharla flashed her best coy smile at him and walked away."

Finally, she leaves me in peace, Tavan thought. The last thing he truly cared about just now was whom his sister would marry. He grabbed a halter off the corral fence post, whistled for his horse and waited until the white mare came to him. He slipped the bit into her mouth, the leather straps over her head and positioned the reins where they needed to be. Next, he grabbed a handful of mane, swung up and headed toward the farmlands. This time his brothers were not tagging along and he was relieved.

*

Sharla rejoined her friend Jenae near the cottages, and together they watched Tavan ride up the path to the adjoining glen. "I hear he fancies Kristin," said Jenae.

"Where did you hear that?"

"I heard Callum swear his wife to secrecy, just before he told her. 'Tis Kristin Tavan fancies."

"Kristin? She does not suit Tavan well at all. She is a farm lass and he should have a wife who is accustomed to the village."

"What difference could that make?"

Sharla rolled her eyes. "You know very well what difference it makes. A farm lass is often dirty where a village lass keeps herself clean. That is not something one learns unless taught from birth."

"All MacGreagors keep the laws of being clean so an enemy cannot smell them." She watched the faraway look in Sharla's eyes for a moment. "You mean he should marry someone like you? You have chosen him?"

"I might have, but you must swear not to breathe a word. I will have your head if you do."

Jenae looked down, spotted a piece of wool lint and brushed it off her skirt. "I am as bonnie as you, perhaps he will prefer me."

"You fancy Tavan?"

"Why not, if he is good enough for you, he is…"

"He will not choose you."

"Why not?"

"Because…because he will choose me instead."

"Do you care to place a wager on that?" asked Jenae.

"I do. What shall we wager?"

"A day's washing would suite me fine. I hate doing the wash."

"Agreed."

For Jenae, the challenge was too good to pass up. She was becoming far less impressed with Sharla, than she had been years ago when they first became friends. Sharla's schemes rarely worked, though Sharla managed not to notice and that could easily work to Jenae's advantage. Now, all she had to do to win the wager was to let Sharla embarrass herself in front of Tavan. Easily done, easily done indeed.

*

In the adjoining glen, Tavan looked for Kristin near the small village, but she was not there. If she was helping with the milking, the cow was somewhere in the forest and she had not bothered to bring it out. He took the path over the hill, tied his horse to a tree where he first saw her, and began to make his way through the trees.

After a time, he paused, bent down and examined the undergrowth. It needed more water, which meant the danger of fire remained, but at least yesterday's rain did not come with lightning.

The wild and thorny blackberry bushes might not yield as much fruit, but the late blooming Rhododendron, Rosebay and morning glory appeared on their way to recovery. In fact, the forest looked and smelled like the renewal of life.

He could hardly hear it at first, and was not certain where it was coming from, so he quietly turned around and listened. It was not singing exactly, and it was not the sound he imagined twenty angels would make either, but it was humming and the voice was clearly that of a woman. Cautiously, he followed the sound, taking one quiet step at a time. Stories abounded of men sounding like a woman in an effort to lure an unsuspecting warrior into a trap. Having been captured once before, Tavan was not about to let that happen again.

He paused, crouched down and parted the leaves of a bush so he could see. It was a woman, it was in fact Kristin, and she was humming while picking berries off a bush and putting them in a basket. He couldn't help but listen a while longer. She did indeed have a wonderful voice.

Tavan leaned down, chose a rhododendron in full bloom and finally walked out from behind the bush. He feared he might startle her, but when she saw him she returned his smile. "My mother says every lad should give a lass flowers," he said, handing the flower to her.

She accepted it and then wrinkled her brow. "You have come to give me a flower?"

"I came to thank you. You cooled my face when I needed it most." She simply nodded, so he continued. "I wish to hear more of your singing. My brothers said it was pleasing and now I know 'tis true. Perhaps you might sing for us some evening."

"Perhaps."

"Can you forgive me for not knowing who you are?"

"I will try." She put the flower in her small basket, and then went back to picking berries. "I watch you sometimes."

"Do you?"

"Do you prefer Sharla?"

"Sharla…let me see, is she the one with golden hair or hair the color of rusted iron?"

"She is the one you were talking to last night."

He was surprised Kristin was there, he didn't see her. "Oh *that* Sharla. I tell you true, my mother had to tell me who she was. I fear I am not good with names or faces." He dared to come a little closer and began to help her pick berries.

"Sharla prefers you, I think."

"Sharla is bothersome, but if you repeat what I said, I will deny it."

Kristin giggled. "She would not believe it anyway."

"You know her well?"

"Not well. Why have you not taken a wife?"

Tavan rolled his eyes. "You sound like my father. He is constantly pestering me to marry." Tavan suddenly remembered something. "Have you married?"

"Nay."

"Why not, you are as pleasing as any other lass."

She slowly turned to look in his eyes. "Name three."

"Three what?"

"Three lasses you think are pleasing."

He let his eyes slowly drift to one side. "I fear I cannot."

"Because you do not think them pleasing, or because you cannot remember their names?"

"Both." Too late, he realized his mistake. He should have named her as one. "I mean…"

She patted his arm as if he was a little boy and moved on to the next bush. "Shall I say you do not find any of our lasses pleasing?"

"For my Father's sake, I pray you do not. He enjoys guessing which I will choose."

"You have my word, for I could not bear it."

"Bear what?"

"Living in a place surrounded by so many broken hearts."

Tavan rolled his eyes again. "You mock me and cleverly so. What about you? Have you let the lads approach you in the courtyard yet?"

The next bush was far more heavily laden with fruit, but the berries were not as large, nor as ripe, so she moved to the one beside it. "Not yet. I would like to marry someday, but he must be a very good lad, as good as my father or I will not have him."

"Sadly, you may have a long wait. Never have I heard an unkind word spoken against Samuel."

"He is the very best of lads. Tell me about Mackinzie. I do not have a mother and do not know yours well. What does she do? I mean, how does she fill her time?"

"Well, she does her sewing mostly. She has many friends who bring their mending and sit with her. She gossips and…"

"Your mother gossips?"

"Aye, my mother is the worst of the lot. Tell my mother a secret and you've told the world."

Kristin giggled. She glanced down, realized her basket was almost full and held it out for him to finish the picking. "Father rarely has time to gossip, but he tells me what I need to know. Mostly what I learn comes from the wives of the other farmers."

Tavan's grin lit up his whole face. "Who gets it from someone in the village, who gets it from *my mother*."

Kristin returned his smile and then pondered his remark for a moment. "Perhaps I know your mother better than I thought."

"No doubt you do. Now, it is I who wishes to ask a question. "Why did you lie to my brothers?"

"When? I do not lie."

"Ah, but you do?"

She was shocked. "I do not."

"Did you not say you had seven brothers and eleven sisters?"

She thought for a moment. "I believe it was six brothers and four sisters, or perhaps it was four brothers and six sisters. I can never keep my lies straight."

"Then you admit you lie."

"I admit nothing of the kind. Besides, your brothers know I have no brothers and sisters, so it was not truly a lie."

It was the first time Tavan realized he'd been set up and he intended to have a word with Callum and Patrick as soon as he returned home. "I see, did they also tell you to wash my face?"

"Your face was burned and I took pity. I needed no one to tell me to." She noticed his face was not as bright red as it had been before.

At the same time, he noticed her face was not burned at all, her eyes were a beautiful blue and strands of her blonde hair glistened in sunlight streaming through the trees. He did not mean to stare, but he could not seem to help himself. "It appears my brothers believe I need help finding a wife." At last, he managed to look away. "I suspect my father put them up to it."

*

The day was going well in the MacGreagor keep. To feed the clan during the drought, older cattle had been slaughtered, therefore the men did little hunting and they were eager to get back to it. There was gossip to be had out there in the woods, there always was, and a world without gossip was intolerable. It was also time to clean out the storehouses and prepare for the next harvest. Sawney assigned men to take care of that task, and was about to make other assignments, when the door opened and one of the guards entered.

Sawney knew by the expression on the man's face, the news was not meant for all to hear. He glanced at his wife and the women with her near the hearth, stood up, motioned for the guard to follow and went up the stairs to the second floor. He waited for the man to enter the bedchamber and then closed the door. "What is it?"

"Buchannans."

"Where?"

"Two hours at most. They are coming here."

"How do you know?" asked Sawney

"A Haldane heard them talking about it when they crossed their land."

"How many?"

"The one who wears many jewels and thirty or so with him. The Haldane could not get a good count," the guard answered.

"Laird Buchannan wears many jewels."

"Aye, he does. I saw him last spring."

"Did the Haldane learn why they are coming?"

"Nay."

"In all these years, we have heard nothing from the Buchannan. Why now?" Sawney ran the fingers of one hand through his hair, turned and walked to the window. A thousand reasons ran through his mind, but only one seemed important enough to bring Laird Buchannan to the MacGreagor glen. Arabella was dead and Buchannan somehow knew her secret. If it was true, they were likely headed for a fierce and bloody clan war.

At length he turned back around. "Tell the guards to let them pass and to give but one short whistle when they reach the glen." He watched the guard nod, leave, and then heard him walk down the stairs.

Sawney didn't have long to make his plans. "Arabella," he whispered. "What have you done now?"

*

Sawney could not remember a man in his youth who did not dream of Arabella. The truth be told, he once preferred her himself, yet his father would not have approved. Fortunately, Sawney met Mackinzie and married her instead, or he might have found himself drawn in by Arabella's wickedness. It was fortunate for him, but not for the man Arabella finally chose. It was not fortunate for that man at all, and if she was truly dead, she had somehow managed to reach back from the grave to torture her husband yet again.

He abruptly turned and went back downstairs. Even the women were now standing at the bottom waiting to hear what was happening, and there was no way to avoid them. "Buchannan's are coming and we know not why."

Sawney calmly looked around and then walked to the center of the room. Tavan was not there and if ever he needed his second in command, it was now. Instead, he turned to Alec, his third. "All the lads are to take their families into the woods and hide them. See they take ample water and food with them. We have but one hour to prepare. After, tell the lads to take up positions around the glen, but to stay hidden unless I give the signal. We must not attack first? I will see what Laird Buchannan wants of us first."

*

Kristin liked Tavan even more now that he was speaking to her. She had given him ample opportunity to notice her, but it took putting her face just a few inches from his to get him to truly see her. If what her father said was true, finding herself attracted to him was not enough - she had to like him as well. And, if his brothers and father were willing to help, she was grateful, for she truly did like Tavan.

Tavan, on the other hand, was concerned. He had not meant to imply that he might choose her for a wife, even if his family encouraged it, and hoped she did not take it that way. After all he knew very little about her. At least that was something he could remedy. "Tell me, what happened to your mother?"

When he reached for more berries, she put her hand on his to stop him. "The basket is full." She watched him toss the ones in his hand into his mouth and smiled. "My mother died when I was small."

"I am sorry to hear that."

Kristin began to walk back through the forest. "Father said she was wonderful and he loved her very much. He must have, he never married again even though I encouraged it. He should have another wife, now that I am old enough to marry. I will regret leaving him all alone."

He waited until she looked at him. "Shall we conspire to find him a wife?"

Kristin tipped her head to one side. "I doubt you would be any good at that, unless you somehow managed to remember the names of all the lasses after all." She looked away for a moment and then looked back. "In all these years, I wonder why Sawney never married Father off."

"I wonder too. It is not like my father to forget a lad in need of a wife." It was indeed very curious and Tavan was perplexed by it. Not once had he heard his father mention Samuel as a good match for a woman. It was very, very odd.

"There is one lass who might do. I see her sometimes talking to father. Her name is Sile and she is always very pleasant to me. She would make a good farmer's wife."

"Why do you say that?"

"I am not certain, 'tis just a feeling. I like her, although the clan pays little attention to her. When she comes, the dogs run to greet her as if she were a long lost friend. Father says that those the dogs like, the other animals will also abide. What can we do to bring Sile and my father together?"

Tavan liked this little conspiracy. It would give him ample reasons to come see Kristen and something to look forward to. If his father could be a good matchmaker, so could he. "Well, first we must…"

*

Except for the birds in the trees, and the thunder of the horse's hooves, there was complete silence in the MacGreagor glen when Laird Buchannan and his men entered. They proudly rode sleek horses of every color. The men wore dark blue kilts, matching shirts and carried large, round shields to fend off arrows if the MacGreagors chose to fight. No whistles sounded the alarm and no people showed their faces, yet Hendry Buchannan could feel MacGreagor warriors on all sides of the glen watching from behind the trees and the cottages.

Fearing an attack, Hendry held up a hand and slowed his warriors. The MacGreagors, he had heard, were fierce warriors few dared to challenge, and although it was a mistake to show fear, it would also defeat his purpose if it appeared they came to do more than talk.

Slowly and deliberately, Hendry led his men up the long glen and at last, he spotted a man standing alone in front of the village. The fully armed man stood with his legs apart and his hands clasped behind his back in a non-threatening manner. It was a good sign the MacGreagors were not looking for a fight either. Laird Buchannan motioned for his men to stop, dismounted and handed his reins to Michael, his second in command. Then he too clasped his hands behind his back and began to close the distance between he and the man who waited to greet him. When he was only a few feet away, he stopped.

Sawney studied the man with rugged looks, a squared jaw and blond hair. Just as he had heard, Laird Buchannan was adorned with jewels in layers of necklaces and bracelets. More were embedded in his belt and in the top of his shoes. "I am laird Sawney MacGreagor."

Hendry looked his opponent up and down. They were the same height and weight, although Sawney was clearly the younger man. The MacGreagor wore no jewels and for a moment, he wondered if Sawney had taken off his jewels intending to fight. "You are not as big as I have heard."

"Nor are you." It was good to break the ice and Sawney breathed a little easier.

"Arabella is dead."

Sawney lowered his eyes. "I am grieved to hear it."

His eyes were blazing when Hendry confessed, "I am not. I have come for the child."

They were the words Sawney feared most and the fate of hundreds rested on what he said in return. "Arabella told you?"

"With her dying breath. I thought to kill her, but she died before I could."

For a man used to expressing himself with his hands, it was difficult for Sawney to keep them clasped behind his back. Yet bringing them forward would alert his men and one wrong move could drench the whole glen in blood. "The...child does not know."

"I see. Tell me, is it a laddie or a lassie?"

"'Tis a lass of seventeen."

Abruptly, Laird Buchannan unclasped his hands and took a shocked step back. Behind him, the Buchannans moved their hands a little closer to the handle of their swords. Laird MacGreagor, they suspected, could easily take their laird and even if they did not like the man, no other clan had the right to cut their laird down.

Michael, a husky man with dark blond hair and brown eyes, slowly scanned the edge of the trees. The absence of people made him wary, but he understood it. No doubt the women and children were on the other side of a hill, protected by women who could fight as well as men. Which hill, he could not guess. He listened, but heard no sounds of frightened children or crying babies. It was quiet...frighteningly quiet.

The MacGreagor warriors held their breaths as well. They were grateful Laird Buchannan put a distance between him and his men. If Sawney chose to fight and struck his opponent down, they were certain they could fully protect him, before the Buchannans had time to charge. For most of the MacGreagors, it was the first time they had experienced the terror of a possible war, and tensions were high as each watched for the first sign of a battle.

Hendry struggled to regain his wits. "Seventeen?" He remembered himself and clasped his hands behind his back again to calm his men. "Arabella said our first child did not draw breath. Instead, she brought her here? Why, MacGreagor, why did she do it?"

"I do not know." Sawney took a deep breath and let it out. "Perhaps a spot of wine?"

Sharing a flask of wine would ease all the warriors and Hendry quickly agreed. He watched Sawney very slowly bring his hands forward, untie his flask and hand it to him. Then he took a long swallow and handed it back. He felt the liquid warm his stomach and never had he needed it more. At least now there would be no need to keep his hands behind him.

Sawney took a swallow, shoved the stopper in place and then tied his flask back. "'Tis not the worst of it."

What could be worse, Hendry wondered. Just the same, he took a moment to prepare himself before he asked, "What?"

"Arabella's husband did *not* set her aside."

Laird Buchannan searched for the truth in Sawney's unyielding expression, finally looked down and shifted his eyes from side to side. "I have lived with her all these years in sin?" He brought a hand up to his brow and closed his eyes. There seemed to be no end to Arabella's deceit.

Once more, Sawney waited for his opponent to get beyond his shock. "I too, am to blame. I could have come to you when we heard you were to marry."

"What stopped you?"

"Would you have believed me?"

Hendry knew the answer to that question. He wanted her so badly, he would not have believed the Pope. "I am shamed to confess the power she had over me. Not once did I suspect her lies. Why did her husband not call me out?"

"Arabella loved you and not him. I could not make her come back, nor was he willing to force her. He knew he could not keep her long if he did, yet..."

"Yet what?"

"He hoped she would come back someday."

"He would have forgiven her?"

"Love makes a lad do stupid things."

Hendry almost laughed. "How well I am learning." It was no laughing matter and he reminded himself getting his child...his daughter had to be foremost on his mind. "Arabella gave me five sons, all lost. She was all I had...until now."

"The lass is all Arabella's husband has. Do I hurt one lad to ease the pain of another? I cannot. Arabella's husband is a MacGreagor and my clan would never forgive me."

Each time Sawney mentioned Arabella's husband, he could see the mixture of pain and anger in Buchannan's eyes. "What will you do?"

"I have a daughter kept from me all her life. What would you do?"

"I feared you might ask that. I truly do not know." He could see no way out and needed time to think. "She is a lot like her mother. She loves the forest, wanders about for hours, and sings with a voice sent from heaven. Most of all, she loves the lad she calls Father. Shall we hurt her, you and I? Is not the price she will pay for her mother's lies too high?"

"Surely, you do not ask me to go home without her. She is my flesh and blood. I can give her far more than a farmer."

Sawney could feel his temper rising. "That farmer gave her care when she was ill. He watched her grow, made certain she was well fed and taught her to love the land and the animals on it. He gave her everything he could: all the while knowing his wife was in your arms and your bed."

Hendry instantly looked away from Sawney's piercing eyes.

There was nothing he could do to right that wrong after all these years, and he was not about to debate it with anyone now. Instead, he again reminded himself he was only there to get his child. "How long have you known about her?"

"All her life."

"Do others know?"

"It was hardly a secret at the time, but no one talks of it now."

Hendry looked back at his men. Arabella must have had help, but who in his very own clan hated him enough to keep a child from him? For now, however, it mattered not and he turned his attention back to Sawney. "She does not know?"

"'Twas up to Samuel to tell her, but he has not and until now, no one cared. The MacGreagors love Kristin and will not easily give her up. What then...do we fight?"

"I did not come here to fight."

"But you will, if you have to?"

"She is my blood, MacGreagor, she belongs with me."

Sawney had used every argument he could think of, and now he needed to come up with a peaceful solution. At length he said, "MacGreagors do not force lasses to go or stay. There is but one thing to do...let Kristin decide. If she refuses to go with you, will you abide by her choice?"

Hendry Buchannan was used to having his way in all things. Therefore, agreeing to let his daughter decide was not easy. Why would she come away with a stranger instead of staying with a loving father? Still, it seemed the only reasonable solution for now, so he nodded his consent and prayed he would not regret his decision.

"We should go to her alone, just the two of us," said Sawney. "If we frighten Kristin, she will go into the forest and we may never find her." He held his breath and then released it when Laird Buchannan nodded. He had no idea what Samuel would do, and if Samuel managed to kill Laird Buchannan somehow, Sawney did not want the Buchannan warriors to see it.

While Hendry walked back to his men, Sawney called for his horse, mounted, and waited. He watched laird Buchannan speak to his warriors, retrieve his horse, and then ride toward him. Slowly, Sawney led the way down the path to the adjoining glen.

CHAPTER IV

Neither the MacGreagors nor the Buchannans were happy to see their lairds ride off alone, but there was nothing they could do about it. Gordon MacGreagor waited a few minutes and then cautiously stood up. He slowly moved away from his hiding place behind a tall headstone in the graveyard, and just as his laird had, he clasped his hands behind his back to show he meant no aggression. On days when there was little work to do, he often fished in a pond not far from the land of the Buchannan, which is where he and Michael Buchannan became trusted friends. This day, there was gossip to be had and Gordon meant to hear it from Michael first hand.

Happy to see Gordon, Michael dismounted and motioned for the other Buchannans to do the same. It had been difficult to keep Arabella's death a secret from the other clans, but Laird Buchannan gave him the task and he was curious to see if the Buchannans had obeyed him.

Relieved that there would be no war just now, Callum and Patrick also revealed their hiding places and followed Gordon into the glen. As they walked, Patrick whispered to his brother, "Where is Tavan?"

"I do not know, but he will hear it if we fight and come soon enough."

"I pray you are right." He glanced around, saw other MacGreagors show themselves and begin to walk into the glen. By then, the Buchannans had laid down their shields and gathered behind Michael.

"What is it?" Gordon asked as soon as the two men were close enough to talk. "What has happened?"

"You have not heard?" Michael asked. He was happy to see his friend shake his head. "Arabella is dead." His announcement seemed to echo across the glen as MacGreagors shared the news with other curious MacGreagors.

Gordon felt a twinge of regret, but it passed quickly enough. "Did he ever catch her?"

"Nay, he had a blind eye where she was concerned," Michael answered.

"Who is Arabella?" Patrick asked.

Michael was surprised he didn't know. "She is…was the blight on the soul of a thousand lads."

"A thousand?" Callum scoffed, moving to stand on the other side of Gordon.

Gordon shook his head. "I am not sorry she is gone."

"Nor are most of us," said Michael. "I can guess, but do you know why Hendry comes to you now, after all these years?"

Gordon hesitated to say anything, but they would all know soon enough anyway. "Aye, he has come for Kristin."

"Kristin?" both Patrick and Callum asked at the same time.

"Who is Kristin?" Buchannan asked.

"She is his daughter. Arabella swore she would not tell, but I suspect she has broken that pledge," said Gordon.

"Kristin is Samuel's daughter." Patrick argued. He was beginning to get a sickening feeling in the pit of his stomach.

If anyone knew the truth, it was the elder Gordon MacGreagor and it was time the truth was told finally. He remembered all too well what happened. "I've a story to tell and 'tis not a pleasant one." He glanced around, realized other men were drawing near and took a deep breath. Then he began, "Arabella married…"

*

Laird MacGreagor led the way down the path beside the gardens to the floor of the valley. He wanted to give Samuel as much warning as he could, although the moment Samuel saw the Buchannan, he would suspect what was happening. The only question was, would Samuel put up a fight?

What Sawney saw next both surprised and bothered him. At the edge of the forest, he spotted Kristin and Tavan was with her. Of all the young women Tavan could have for the asking, Kristin would be Sawney's last choice. It made this horrible situation that much worse, especially if she chose to go with the Buchannans and Tavan was not willing to give her up.

After Arabella abandoned Samuel, Sawney should have banished her. If he had, she would not have brought Kristin here and this misery could have been avoided. He was a young laird when it happened and now, it was far too late to regret long ago decisions.

*

Samuel MacGreagor stepped out of his cottage at the southern edge of the glen and looked up at the sky. It promised to be a clear afternoon and he had much to do. The milking was finished, other chores were done and next, he needed to count the cows and see that none were lost in the night. After that, he... Two men were slowly riding toward him and one made him draw in a sharp breath. "Buchannan," he whispered. He scanned the edge of the forest hoping to spot his daughter, and caught just a glimpse of her standing next to Tavan. He was about to shout a warning when he thought better of it.

Samuel tried to calm his nerves. Perhaps Buchannan was here for some other reason and they would pass him by. After all, Sawney would not be without his guard if something was wrong...

Something *was* wrong. Sawney put his hand over the patch of MacGreagor cloth that covered his heart. It was a sign the MacGreagors used, when all was not as it seemed. "Arabella," Samuel muttered. He did not want to hear it, but he knew. Deep down, he knew she was dead and hung his head. She would not be coming back to him...not ever, and his heart was beginning to break. Once more he looked for Kristin and when he did not see her, he prayed she would stay hidden.

"Arabella," Samuel whispered again. "Have you betrayed us?" He took another deep breath, opened his eyes and waited for what he feared most.

Still several yards away, Sawney halted his horse, dismounted, waited for Laird Buchannan to do the same, and together they walked to where Samuel was waiting. Sawney wished he knew of a gentler way of saying it, but at least it was better coming from him than from Laird Buchannan. "Arabella has passed." He watched Samuel bow his head and gave him a moment to collect his thoughts, before he said the rest. "Laird Buchannan has come for his daughter."

"Nay!" Samuel shouted. He glared at the stranger with a

fierceness he did not know he possessed, put his hand on his sword and began to draw it.

Sawney quickly grabbed Samuel's arm. "Will you let Kristin see you die?"

"He will not have her. I will not allow it!"

*

Too far away to hear, Kristin stood just inside the forest and wrinkled her brow. "What is happening?"

"I do not know. 'Tis the first time I have seen a Buchannan in our glens," said Tavan.

She didn't take her eyes off her father when she answered, "I have seen one often enough."

"Have you? Who?"

"Her name is Arabella and she is my father's sister."

"I did not know Samuel has a sister. Do you like her?"

"I suppose I do. She has an odd way of looking at me. I do not stay in the cottage long when she comes. Father prefers it when I leave them alone to talk. What they could possibly have to talk about is beyond me."

"Does Samuel go to see her?"

Kristin looked puzzled. "Come to think of it, he has never left this valley save to search for a lost calf or lamb. Nay, he has never once gone off to see her. I never before realized how odd that is. Aunt Arabella does not speak of a husband or any children, so I suppose since she is willing to come here, he finds no reason to go to her. …That must be it."

Tavan carefully watched the three men standing outside Samuel's cottage. Whatever they were discussing, it was not good news and it was clearly upsetting Samuel.

"Shall we go see what is happening?" Kristin asked.

"Not yet. Wait until we see what they do." He was both surprised and pleased when she slipped her hand into his. "Are you frightened?"

"A little. Do you know this Buchannan?" she asked.

"Not well. He is laird and wears many jewels. It is said he will kill a lad for looking at his wife too long. I do not doubt it, he is as big as my father, perhaps bigger."

She moved a little closer and when he dropped her hand in favor of putting his arm around her, she welcomed his comfort. "Father is furious, I fear he will fight."

Tavan watched Sawney move to stand between the two men. "There, you see, my Father will not let them fight."

"I doubt he can prevent it, Sawney is but one lad."

Before he could stop her, Kristin pulled away and began to run into the valley. "Kristin, come back, it is not…" he shouted. There was little he could do but go after her, and by the time he caught up and pulled her to a stop, she had attracted the attention of the farmers in the fields, her father, Sawney and Laird Buchannan. Tavan knew if he gave the signal, all the farmers would come running, but the look on Sawney's face told him not to.

He grabbed Kristin's shoulders and turned her until she faced him. "Stop."

"But I…"

"I command you to stop. 'Tis not safe."

She had forgotten he was second in command, let her shoulders slump and nodded.

"You will not put yourself between lads who are set to fight, agreed?"

"Agreed."

Laird Buchannan's mouth slowly fell open. Kristin was the exact image of Arabella, and he could hardly believe what he was seeing. Dozens must have seen the resemblance, yet none mentioned it to him. He had clearly been betrayed by more than one and for a second time, his ire was raised. At last, the MacGreagor Kristin was with let her slowly approach, and he could not take his eyes off his daughter as she came closer and closer.

As was customary, Kristin curtsied to Sawney and then waited to be introduced. "Kristin, this is Laird Buchannan," Sawney finally remembered to say.

She smiled at the giant of a man standing next to her laird and then curtsied to him as well. "You are welcome here." It was then she noticed the worried look on her father's face, forgot Tavan's command and quickly went into her father's arms, "You look as though someone stole your horse, Father, what is the matter with you?"

"Arabella died."

"Oh no, I feared that was it." Kristin hugged her father again. "I know how much you loved her, and how you hated to see your sister go each time she came. I once heard you ask her to stay, but she would not. How did she die?"

Samuel could hardly catch his breath. There were so many lies to explain and he had no idea where to start.

"She died of a grave illness," Laird Buchannan softly said. He was surprised Kristin knew her mother at all, even as her aunt.

Still in Samuel's arms, Kristin turned to Laird Buchannan. He was not an unpleasant looking man, as she thought some men surely were. He had no hideous scars, his beard was neatly trimmed and his eyes did not make her uncomfortable, though he did seem to be staring at her a bit too long. She remembered hearing that the Buchannans fought the MacGraw not too long ago, and found it surprising he had no scars. "Were you with her?"

"Aye," Hendry answered.

"Then I thank you for seeing to her. Have you come to take us to the burial?"

"Nay, she is already buried."

"Oh, I see. Then we have you to thank for that as well. Laird Buch…"

"Kristin, I…there is something you do not know," Samuel tried.

"Well let me see, I know how to shoe a horse, how to ride and how to find my way home when I am lost. I also know…"

"Kristin."

"What Father?"

Tavan stayed a few steps away…far enough away so he would have room to draw his sword if need be. He tried to read what his father was thinking, but Sawney kept his eyes on Kristin instead of Laird Buchannan. It was a good sign, he supposed.

Samuel took a deep breath. "Kristin, I have always loved you. You believe that, do you not?"

"Of course I believe it, you are my father." She could feel his tension and it was beginning to alarm her. "Father, what is it? What can the matter be?"

He gripped both her arms and made her step back. "Kristin, I am not your father!"

She searched his eyes for a moment and then giggled. 'Tis a very fine jest, Father, but..."

"'Tis not a jest. Laird Buchannan is your true father."

She stared into Samuel's eyes for what seemed ceaseless moments before she dropped her gaze. "You are not my father?"

"Nay, I tell you true, Laird Buchannan is your father."

Kristin abruptly turned, glanced at Laird Buchannan, dismissed him and went to Tavan. "You are still Tavan, are you not, or have I gone daft?"

Tavan exchanged worried looks with his father and then took her in his arms to protect her from the pain she was about to feel. "You are not daft."

"Perhaps not, but someone here has lied to me all my life. Which one, do you guess, or do I blame both my fathers?" She turned in his arms, faced Samuel and tightened her fists. "Well, what happened? Why am I his daughter now,? Have you given me away?"

"Kristin," said Sawney, "Calm yourself."

She turned her glare on him. "If Laird Justin suddenly claimed you were not his son, could you be calm?"

"Kristin," Sawney began to command. "I am your laird and you will keep silent and let me explain." He patiently waited until she finally nodded. "Good. It was your mother who gave you up. Samuel claimed you, and loved you as well as any father could, yet 'tis not his blood you carry."

"May I speak now?"

"Nay, you will wait. Lest you blame him, Laird Buchannan did not know about you until a few days ago. He has come to ask you to go home with him, but the choice is yours. He will not force you, nor will I."

She hardly noticed when Tavan tightened his arms around her. "Now may I speak?"

"If you must," Sawney said.

"Is it true, Father? My mother did not die, she gave me up instead?"

"Please, Kristin, let me explain. Your mother..." Samuel started.

"Where is this mother of mine who did not want me?"

Samuel closed his eyes and uttered a truth he had not yet fully accepted. "She died."

"Good, then I am saved the trouble of killing her."

Samuel was shocked. "Kristin, why do you talk like this? You never have before."

"I never felt myself drowning before." Kristin wanted to cry, but she was too furious. Then a thought occurred to her. She narrowed her eyes and glared at Samuel. "What was my mother's name? I never thought to ask that before."

Samuel looked to be in such pain, Sawney decided to answer for him. "Arabella was your mother."

Kristin nearly laughed. "Arabella? My aunt was my mother, my father is now my uncle, and this stranger wants to take me away. How very fortunate I am. Next you will say my name is not Kristin." She put the tips of her fingers on both sides of her head as though it was about to burst. 'Tis too much."

Samuel desperately tried to find the right words. "I am not your uncle. I am…"

Hendry was amazed at how much Kristin sounded like her mother. She even had Arabella's same temper; a temper Hendry often enjoyed calming. Just then, something Kristin said finally hit home, and he abruptly turned to Samuel. "My wife came here often?"

"*Your* wife?" Samuel shot back, "She was *my* wife!"

Hendry quickly returned Samuel's fierce tone of voice. "She said you set her aside."

"She lied!"

Kristin began to go weak in the knees and could not help slumping against Tavan. Her disbelieving eyes fell on Sawney, the one of the three men she still trusted. "My mother was a bigamist?"

Sawney lowered his eyes. "Aye."

"How long have you known?" she asked.

"Since the beginning," Sawney answered.

"Does everyone know?"

Sawney dared not look at her. The anger in her eyes was becoming hard to look at, and he couldn't blame her. "Not everyone."

This time she felt it when Tavan tightened his arms around her. It served to calm her a little. "Why did no one tell me?"

Sawney answered, "Arabella asked us not to."

It did not take long to get her dander back up. "Arabella…I am learning to hate that name. Arabella left us, Arabella lied to all of us and you kept her secret. What power did she hold?"

It was Hendry who answered. "Your laird did not want to go to war. Arabella was not worth fighting over…not for the MacGreagors."

"You would have fought to have my mother, even though she was another lad's wife?"

Laird Buchannan drew in a forgotten breath. "I thought Samuel set her aside."

Kristin's fierceness seemed to increase as she glared at Hendry. "For what cause? Adultery with you?"

Sawney squared his shoulders. "Enough Kristin. What is done is done. If you must place the blame, place it on your mother."

Tavan was almost as confused as Kristin, and since he was the only one she was not furious with, he thought he might be able to help. "Perhaps we should take a walk until you have calmed."

"Nay, Tavan, I have questions still."

"Then you will ask them quietly," said Sawney.

Kristin glanced toward the other cottages and realized all the farmers, as well as their families, were watching. Thoroughly embarrassed, she bowed her head. "I did not mean to shout. May I ask my questions?"

"Aye," Sawney answered.

"If my mother was married to my father, then how do you know who my blood father is?"

Sawney did not have the answer to that question and looked at Samuel.

Samuel truly considered adding one more lie, a lie that would keep Kristin with him, but he could not be certain Arabella had not told Laird Buchannan the truth. "Because your mother was not with me that year complete."

Kristin did not like his answer, but there it was. She probably was Laird Buchannan's daughter, as dreadful as that seemed. She looked at each of the men standing before her, decided she had no more questions and turned in Tavan's arms. "I will take that walk with you now."

*

In front of the main MacGreagor village, both the Buchannans and the MacGreagors were captivated by Gordon's story. Few knew all the details and the younger men knew nothing at all. Of course, even after Gordon told what he knew, they did not know everything, how could they? Still, they knew enough and Patrick often exchanged worried looks with his brother. "We must tell Tavan."

"Tavan?" Gordon asked. "What has he to do with this?"

"Tavan fancies Kristin. We think he aims to marry her," said Callum.

Gordon frowned. "Nay, he must not marry her. She has her mother's blood and her grandmother's before her. No good can come from marriage to such as that...no good whatsoever."

"You cannot mean it is in her blood," said Callum.

"Aye, 'tis in her blood to be sure. Kristin roams the forest the same as her mother and her grandmother. Who is to say why they do that, save it is in their blood. Kristin is wild and free, and no lad shall tame her. Mark my word; she will become another Arabella through and through."

Michael Buchannan took in every word and wondered if the Buchannans could survive another Arabella. At least their laird could not marry this one and make her their mistress. Yet there were plenty of warriors itching to take laird Buchannan on, and one of them might claim Arabella's daughter. On the other hand, if Kristin married a MacGreagor, any MacGreagor, she would not be a problem for the Buchannan. All he needed to do was somehow make that happen. Let the MacGreagors have Arabella this time.

"Who was Arabella's mother?" one of the Buchannans asked.

"Murdina," Gordon answered.

"Murdina?" Callum asked. "I remember hearing about her, she disappeared one day and no one ever saw her again."

Gordon was happy to tell about that too. "Arabella was grown by then. They went off together that morning and Arabella came back alone. She swore she did not know where her mother was, but some said…"

"Arabella killed her own mother?" Michael asked.

Gordon answered, "Murdina was…she was willing and who can say for certain what has become of her?"

"You mean Kristin will be willing too?" asked Patrick. "I care not to believe that. Daughters do not always become like their mothers, nor do sons take after fathers. Besides, Kristin was not raised by a mother who could teach her evil."

Gordon rolled his eyes. "Arabella was here often enough, I have seen her."

"So have I," said several others.

Gordon put his hand on Patrick's shoulder. "There are always lasses who are willing. All lads know who they are and how to find them. They bear children, and who is to say which lad is the father? The lad who marries Kristin will always wonder if his sons are truly his. I would not wish that on a brother of mine, nor would I wish it on Tavan. 'Tis best to keep him clear of Kristin for his own sake."

*

All Sawney, Samuel and Laird Buchannan could do was watch Tavan take Kristin for a walk down the valley. What she decided could affect hundreds of lives and all three men were well aware of it.

Nevertheless, Samuel had questions and at length, he asked Laird Buchannan, "Did she die peacefully?"

"Far more peacefully than she deserved," Hendry answered. "When did you see Arabella last?"

"A few weeks ago. I suspected she was dying then."

"Was nothing she said the truth?"

Samuel couldn't help but smirk. There was more than one way to shove a dagger in the man's stomach and twist it so it would hurt more. "Not that I am aware of. I did not know she was bedding you until the day she left me. Later, she came to my bed when she needed more than you could give her." Samuel watched his words make Laird Buchannan's blood begin to boil and he was glad. The man deserved that and more. He thought Buchannan might draw his sword and in a way, he hoped they would fight.

Hendry wanted nothing more than to strike Samuel dead, but instead, he took two deep breaths and calmed himself. It was an insult he would not soon forget, but he was well aware the MacGreagors in the glen outnumbered him. He would not live long if he killed Samuel. Revenge for this insult too, he could save for later. Just now he wanted to know the full extent of Arabella's treachery. "Were there other lads?"

"There were rumors."

Sawney remembered to breathe. If they were going to fight, Samuel's words surely would have started it. Secretly, he was proud of the way Samuel was handling the situation and took note to say so later. He could hardly wait to tell Mackinzie all about it when they retired for the night. Tavan kept his wits about him too and it did not go unnoticed by his father. Perhaps Tavan would make a good laird after all. Of course, the danger still remained that Tavan might interfere, if Kristin decided to go.

Hendry drew in another calming breath. "Arabella came to you to give birth?"

"Nay, she came after." Samuel paused for a moment to recall exactly what happened. "She meant to arrive before, but the child came too soon. She sat on her horse covered in blood and I ran to her, but instead of letting me pull her down, she handed me the babe and sped off. She had not tied Kristin's cord and she was bleeding. I yelled, 'Why Arabella, why,' but she did not answer.

Hendry shook his head in disgust. "Stupid lass, I would have loved a daughter."

"Stupid perhaps, but not void of all feeling. She loved Kristin as best she knew how," said Samuel.

"Why did you not come to kill me when I took Arabella from you?"

"I would have lost." Samuel kept his eyes on Kristin as he continued, "I have hated you every day for eighteen years."

There was little Laird Buchannan could say to that. "If Kristin refuses to go with me, will you allow me to come again?"

Samuel raised an eyebrow, "If Kristin desires it. That is, if she does not slay me in my bed for lying to her. She has her mother's quick temper and she does not forget a wrong."

Buchannan mistakenly chuckled. "I shall remember that."

Samuel had one last twist of the dagger left and turned his glare back on Hendry. "You best remember it well. If she goes with you and even if she comes to love you, she will not forget it was you who took her mother from her."

*

Kristin stopped walking. She spotted a wild flower the hot summer sun had not killed, bent down and picked it. "Did you not say flowers would make me feel better?"

Tavan smiled. "Shall I find more for you?"

"Nay, this one will do. See, it is almost perfect." She held it up so he could examine the blue petals more closely.

"I say it *is* perfect, what fault do you find in it?"

"I find fault with many flowers. It seems God does not make all flowers perfect."

"I suspect He thinks He does."

"I hope not. I search for hours for the perfect flower and the enjoyment would be lost to me. He should keep trying until He gets it right."

"Kristin, is it truly flowers you wish to speak of just now?"

"My mind is too full to consider anything else." She grinned, rose up on tip toe and put her cheek to his. "If I pretend I have not heard it, will it all go away?" She leaned back to see his eyes.

The urge to hold her for a long moment and make her worries go away was nearly unbearable. "I do not believe so."

She let her heels touch the ground again and shrugged. "Did you know?"

"Nay, I have heard nothing of this. But then, I find I know far less than I thought I did."

Her eyes suddenly lit up. "I have it; I shall rid myself of both my fathers and claim yours instead."

"I approve and I am certain my father will as well. Is that your decision then? Will you stay?"

"Must I decide so quickly? A few hours ago I wanted nothing more than to pick berries, but..." She looked down at her empty hands. "What have I done with the basket?"

"I believe we left it in the forest. I will find it for you."

"I thought to bake a pie for him, but I think now Father would not enjoy it. He loved Arabella very much, that much I do know. She must have been quite mad, yet in her madness she must have loved him too...at least a little."

"And you, she kept coming back to see you."

"True. I wonder that she could have left him so easily. Father is a good lad and he would have done all he could to make her happy." Kristin started walking again and remained quiet for a while. "Did you not say Laird Buchannan is wealthy?"

"So I have heard."

"It was for fine things, then." Another idea suddenly crossed her mind and Kristin smiled. "Do you suppose I have brothers and sisters? I should like having a sister very much."

Tavan certainly did not want to be the bearer of more bad news, but what could he do? "I have heard Laird Buchannan lost two sons in their last war."

"Two brothers lost. 'Tis a pity, that one." The string at the end of her braid was starting to slip off and this was the first she noticed. She reached around, pulled her thick braid to the front and took the string out. "My hair matches my father's."

"Aye, it does. Do you wish me to tie it?"

"Nay, I wish the world to go away. I wish we could walk and talk forever, and not have any cause to fret." She tucked the string in her belt, pushed her braid to the back and didn't care if it came undone. She was about to cry and wasn't sure she could prevent it. "Tavan, do you swear to care for Father if I am taken away?"

"No one will take you away unless you wish it so."

"Do you promise?"

"I do." He gave in to his impulse and wrapped his arms around her once more.

"Will the Buchannan forests have perfect flowers?"

Tavan held his breath. "You wish to see for yourself?"

"Perhaps."

"This is your home, we are your family and you belong with us."

Kristin pulled away. "You are my mother's family, the mother who did not want me."

"I make no excuses for her, but the rest of us are not to blame. We have not changed since a few hours ago. We will continue to love you, care for you and provide new shoes when you need them." He hoped the mention of shoes would make her smile, but it didn't.

"You forget one thing. When this day is complete, the

MacGreagors will all know what Arabella has done. How shall I bear the pity in their eyes?"

"I will forbid them to pity you."

She smiled up at him finally. "I do believe you would and I am comforted." She began to walk again, going further away from the men watching behind her. "Perhaps I have sisters."

"Perhaps you could ask."

"Perhaps I shall. I have been as stupid as he. I did not see what was right before my eyes. There were so many signs something was amiss, yet I was as blind as the lad who claims to be my father. You must admit, that one is a stupid, stupid lad."

"Indeed he must be." Tavan suddenly remembered, untied a small cloth sack from his belt, opened it and pulled a carved horse out. "I brought you a gift."

She carefully took it from him and closely examined it. "I shall cherish it forever."

"As well you should. I had a devil of a time getting the horse to stand still."

Kristin giggled. "I would have liked watching that. I shall put this horse on a table in…do you suppose I shall have my own bedchamber if I go to the Buchannans? He is a laird, and perhaps he has many bedchambers, more than Sawney even."

"I suspect he does." Tavan didn't like the way she asked that question, or the look in her eyes just now. She stopped again to look back at her fathers, and when she did, so did he.

CHAPTER V

There seemed to be nothing left to say. Sawney silently watched Kristin with Tavan and patiently waited for her decision. There was a good deal more to Arabella's wickedness, but now was not the time to bring it up. Her passing would be mourned by few, applauded by several MacGreagors, and Sawney was well aware of what could happen if they began to expose all her lies. Now, however, he was more concerned about what his son was thinking. If Kristin was the woman in Tavan's heart, and it appeared she was, he was not likely to let her go.

*

In the MacGreagor village, the women and children began to come out of hiding. They were desperate to know what was happening, but Alec wasn't so sure it was safe. He warned them away with a look of disapproval, but when they began to gather in the courtyard anyway, there was little he could do about it. He decided to go to them and calm their nerves instead.

"Arabella is dead," he whispered to the three nearest him.

"Why have they come here, then?" Sharla asked.

Her mother, Dollag, scoffed. "They have come for Kristin. Her mother is dead finally, and happy am I to hear it."

Sharla had no idea who Arabella was and did not care. If it meant Kristin would be gone, she would have far less competition for Tavan's favors. "Will Sawney let her go?"

Alec did not answer. Instead, he walked back to the men.

When Dollag started to explain it to her daughter, the other women came closer to hear. She told them everything she could remember about Arabella, and then added something new, "After that, Ainsley died." Dollag paused and looked at their faces. For years she silently cursed Arabella for what happened to Ainsley. The day he died, Dollag was forced to lie -- one lie became ten, and then a hundred before the questions stopped. She cared not to live that nightmare again…ever.

"Who was Ainsley?" Sharla asked.

"Never you mind about him." Dollag shook her head and walked away, but every woman heard the name and fully intended to prod their husbands until they knew every detail surrounding the death of Ainsley.

For Sile, there was no joy in the news of Arabella's death. The other women hardly noticed Sile anyway, so she quietly slipped down the path behind the Keep and went back to her cottage. Once she was inside, she closed the door, put her face in her hands and wept.

*

"I have decided," said Kristin. "I shall go with my blood father."

Tavan did not take it well. "You cannot, I forbid it."

She patted his arm as if he was a little boy and tipped her head to one side. "There are two lairds not far away and I doubt either would allow you to prevent it. What upsets you Tavan? Do you worry for my safety? I assure you I can fight as good as any lad."

"Kristin, a lass is not as strong as a lad."

"Aye, but we are more cunning. My father says a red fox is not the only fox a lad must worry about."

He almost smiled. She was right, he could not stop her.

"I shall only stay a fortnight and then I shall come home." She turned and started back.

"And if they do not let you come back? What then?"

"Why would they not let me?"

"Not all clans are the same. We let our lasses come and go as they please, others do not. Your blood father has the power to betroth you to another if he so chooses and you cannot stop him. He is a laird and lairds often marry daughters off to other lairds. They do it to form an alliance. It is done all the time."

She stopped and considered it. "If I am betrothed to you, can he marry me off anyway?"

"Not without starting a war."

"Would the MacGreagors fight to free me?"

"Would you ask them to?"

She didn't have to think that over. "Nay, I would not ask such a thing of the people I love."

He hoped he had finally convinced her, but he was wrong.

"Still, I would like the adventure. Perhaps we can make him give his pledge to bring me home in a fortnight. Do you agree?"

It was easy to see she had made up her mind, and the last thing he wanted to do was cause her more sorrow. He begrudgingly nodded, but he felt a very strong foreboding. The Buchannans were thought to be nearly as well armed and as strong as the MacGreagors, and getting her out, if Laird Buchannan did not keep his pledge, might be impossible.

"Tavan, there is another reason."

"What might that be?"

"Well, if I am gone, the people can have their gossip and be done with it by the time I come back. There will be nothing more to talk about, and you and I can go back to our pleasant lives."

"I can think of nothing I desire more. Will you do this one thing for me, if you are in need, will you send word to me?"

"Aye." She playfully shook her finger at him. "Say you will not start a war, Tavan MacGreagor. I would never forgive you for it. I am not worth the loss of even one MacGreagor."

*

As they watched Kristin and Tavan start back toward them, Sawney tried to distract Arabella's husbands by asking how the Buchannan crops faired in the drought. Hendry only gave yes and no answers without elaborating. He supposed Hendry's mind was too full of what Arabella had done to consider a pleasant conversation. Samuel, on the other hand, was struggling to hold back his grief. Both men couldn't seem to look at anything other than Kristin, but in her manner there was no hint of her decision.

The closer Kristin came, the more she walked and looked like her mother. There was just something about her. Even Sawney was captivated by it and certainly understood his son's attraction to her. Still, she was the kind of woman who could tear his son apart, and he was already thinking of ways to prevent a union between them. He could not read the expression on Kristin's face, but Tavan's was clear. Kristin would agree to go.

Instead of looking at her fathers, Kristin kept her eyes on Sawney until she was close enough to speak. Once more, she curtsied to her laird. "I have decided, but first I must ask you to secure my safety. Ask my blood father to pledge before you, and all of us, that he will bring me back in a fortnight."

"I gladly give my pledge," said Laird Buchannan without waiting for Sawney to ask.

It was the first time Tavan actually looked at the stranger. Buchanan looked honest enough, but all lairds perfected the ability to seem honest, even when they were lying through their teeth. There was no sign of the man's true feelings, just a blankness Tavan could not read.

Samuel shook his head. "Do not trust him, Kristin."

"Father…what do I call you now?"

"He is still your father," Sawney said. "He will always be the one who loved you best."

"You are right. Father it is then, and this other one will be my blood father, agreed?"

Samuel slowly nodded. "But you must…"

"Father, do not fret. I will be back before you have time to miss me." She knew she was hurting him and felt awful about it, but Samuel had her for seventeen years. Now, she was all grown up and it was time for her to taste life. She hugged him again and memorized his loving arms before she went inside their cottage to gather her things. It did not take long. She put a change of clothing in a sack, added her brush and then carefully put the carved horse Tavan gave her inside. When she came out, Samuel was bringing her beige horse around from behind the cottage.

First, she hugged Sawney, then her father once more, and then went into Tavan's arms. She let him hold her for a moment, stepped back and tried to reassure him with a smile. Kristin let Tavan lift her up on her horse and then waited for Sawney and Laird Buchannan to mount their horses. She nodded her readiness, urged her horse forward and followed the men.

Tavan went to stand beside her father, folded his arms and watched her ride away. She looked back at them twice more before she went out of sight. His foreboding was even stronger than before, and he felt as though he might never see her again. At length, he nodded to Samuel and then started down the glen to fetch his horse and Kristin's basket of berries.

When he looked back, Samuel had gone into his cottage and for a moment, Tavan considered staying with him. It was a black day for Samuel, the blackest of all black days, and he did promise Kristin he would watch over her father. Yet Samuel probably needed time alone just now. Nevertheless, there was something he could do, and he walked to the nearest farmer to do it. "Arabella is dead," was all he said.

The farmer nodded. "I thought that must be it. We will see his grief does not overtake him. Is Kristin…?"

"Buchannan promised to return her in a fortnight." Before he was tempted to say he doubted that would happen, Tavan walked away.

*

There was no hiding the surprise on the faces of the Buchannans when they first saw Kristin and Hendry noticed. Perhaps they did not know after all. Her hair had come completely loose and she was as handsome as Arabella had been, perhaps more so. Not one of them said a thing, not even Michael. Her great likeness to Arabella was unnerving and some in Clan Buchannan were not going to be pleased to see her. On Michael's command, the Buchannans separated from the MacGreagors and mounted their horses.

Kristin was mortified. Every MacGreagor was watching her, and never had she felt so self-conscious. What stories they would have to tell, and all of them about her. She had few close friends among the MacGreagors and perhaps now she understood why -- mothers most likely did not want their daughters associating with Arabella's child. Even so, Kristin loved the clan and was always proud to call herself a MacGreagor. Now what was she? She hardly felt like a Buchannan, she felt more like a lost soul set adrift on a sea of confusion. Her father lied, her mother lied, her clan lied and even the laird she loved lied. The only person she could still trust among the MacGreagors was Tavan. In one short afternoon, her attraction to him had become something far more, and suddenly she wasn't so certain she wanted to be without him. Perhaps it was not too late to change her mind.

Laird Buchannan nodded to Sawney before he turned his horse and led Kristin to the warriors waiting in the glen. He halted and then examined the faces of each of his men. "This is my daughter, Kristin, whom you will protect with your lives." None dared deny him, although their nods were anything but enthusiastic. He was about to motion them forward when Kristin abruptly turned her horse around.

She took a long look at the only home she had ever known. Whispers of smoke rose up from cottage chimneys the same as always, and the leaves of the trees twisted and turned in the breeze, but nothing was the same. She might have said a farewell, but the people who should have loved her best stood gawking. She suspected they hoped she might do or say something that would add one more juicy morsel to their wildly anticipated gossip. That, she was determined not to do.

As soon as Kristin turned her horse back around, the Buchannan warriors surround their laird and his daughter, and began the journey home.

*

Sawney dismounted, handed the reins of his horse to a boy and joined the MacGreagors. In silence, every man, woman and child watched the Buchannans until they rode out of sight. It was a relief to see them go and he was pleased his men had made friends with the Buchannan warriors while he was gone. It was much harder to fight a friend than a nameless face known only as the enemy. He said nothing, even when his warriors turned to look at him. They were wise not to question him, for he had not yet decided how much to say.

When he saw the women, including his wife and daughters, standing in the courtyard waiting, he decided he should say something to comfort them. "We are not at war. Kristin is Laird Buchannan's daughter and he has claimed her. She went with him willingly." He walked to her, took his wife in his arms and savored the moment. Then he hugged his daughters and went inside.

An entire flask of wine sounded very good just now, but Sawney settled for a goblet. The last thing he wanted to do was alarm the women in his household. Calm was the order of the day, even though his mind was racing with fears of what was to come. He barely downed half his goblet, before the great hall began to fill with family and friends. They knew not to question him either, but their silence said more than words. He ignored their inquiring eyes, sat at the head of the table and hugged his three grandchildren.

Mackinzie stood behind him and put her hands on his shoulders. "Tavan did not come back."

"I know, he is fine."

"Good."

Sawney had a sudden thought, got up, went back outside and called for his horse.

*

By the time Tavan returned, the MacGreagors were still in the glen. The men were boasting about not being the least bit frightened, while the women confessed to having nearly fainted dead away. Soon after that exchange, the women began prodding the men, but the men seemed unwilling to talk about someone named Ainsley.

Sharla was especially fascinated with her mother's secret and for the most part ignored Jenae. Yet it was Jenae who spotted Tavan coming back first. She turned to watch him and was surprised when he walked his horse toward her, halted and then slid down not two feet away. Unfortunately, by then Sharla had remembered her friend and was right beside her.

Normally, Tavan would have taken his horse to the corral, but as second in command, he thought it was time to keep it in the stable next to his father's. In fact, he decided on the way back it was time to start acting like second in command. He could not remember a time when he had given orders or made decisions without his father handing them down. Today he had. Today he commanded Kristin to stop and she obeyed. It made him understand the power he had, and the wits he would need to have in the future.

Tavan gave his reins to a boy and nodded toward the stable. The boy seemed surprised, but obeyed just the same. It was then he found himself standing between Jenae and Sharla.

"Did you see what happened?" Sharla asked, nearly out of breath. She put her hand over her heart as though it was about to beat out of her chest. "Buchannans in our very glen. I was frightened, I do not mind saying. Sawney said to hide, and hide we did. They were forty of the most gruesome lads I have yet to see."

"And she counted them too," Jenae muttered.

"Tavan," Sharla continued. "Were you in the gardens? We looked, but we did not see you here. I wish to know what happened. Did you see the Buchannan take Kristin away? Surely you saw that, for you came from that direction."

The more she talked, the more annoyed Tavan became. Sharla was the last person he owed an explanation to. Without meaning to, he glared at her and then at Jenae. "Must you know as well?"

Jenae lowered her eyes. "Nay."

"Good." He turned to go, just as Jenae called him back. "What?"

"I am happy you are safe, we need you," Jenae said.

He closed his eyes and relaxed his tense shoulders. "Forgive me, but I do not know your name."

"I am Jenae."

"Thank you, Jenae." He had never noticed her before, but that was nothing new. She had sincere eyes and her voice was far more pleasant than Sharla's. He looked at her a moment longer and then walked toward the courtyard where his father stood waiting.

Tavan did not want to answer all of Sawney's questions either, but there was no way to avoid that. To his surprise, Sawney stopped the boy leading his horse and handed the reins back to Tavan. No words were spoken as they mounted and Sawney led his son away from the clan, across the glen and up the side of the highest hill. Soon, six guards on horseback followed.

*

Kristin was heartsick. Not one of the MacGreagors had wished her well, but then, perhaps some meant to and she had not paused long enough to allow it. Surely, not all of them hated her mother. Now that she was away, she was not certain just how she should act around the Buchannan. Neither happy nor sad seemed appropriate, so she settled on having no expression at all.

Her father, she noticed, rode on ahead and did not look back at her. She was surrounded by strangers...strangers who knew far more about her mother than she did. Thinking of Arabella as her mother instead of her aunt was going to take some getting used to. She felt a little hollow for not taking the time to get to know Arabella better. When they talked, the conversation was pleasant enough, just not very exciting. In fact, she could not remember one single thing they ever talked about.

She could certainly remember the look on her father's face each time Arabella came. It was as though his joy would swallow him up, and then, of course, the sadness he felt for days after she left. All that time, he was her *true* husband. At least now Kristin understood why he wanted to be alone with Arabella when she came.

Samuel was anything but a coward. Kristin once saw him stand directly in front of a charging wild boar, and wait until his aim was perfect, before he let loose his arrow and killed it. Yet he did not call Laird Buchannan out? Stranger still, neither husband killed Arabella in all those years, although both had good reason. Of course, Laird Buchannan...Hendry, did not know of her treachery. Or did he? If he had no hint at all, Kristin was now riding behind the most witless man in all of Scotland. She would call him, Hendry, she decided. The last thing she wanted to do was call an exceedingly stupid man, Father.

From time to time, as they rode toward the Buchannan village, one of her father's warriors looked at her a little too long for her comfort. Perhaps they looked at every woman that way or perhaps they doubted she could stay on a horse. Little did they know.

When the path narrowed to a span wide enough for only two riders, one of the warriors rode next to her. She glanced at him a couple of times, but he appeared to be carefully watching for some sort of surprise attack. The Buchannans had been in a war not too long ago, she remembered, and wondered just how much danger she had put herself in. Perhaps she made her decision far too quickly after all.

"I am Michael Buchannan," the man riding beside her said finally. "I am your father's second in command."

"Why do they stare at me, Michael Buchannan?"

He was surprised she did not know. "'Tis because you look like your mother."

Kristen sometimes noticed a resemblance to her aunt, but never really gave it much thought. No one else ever mentioned it, but then, she didn't think very many of them knew Arabella came to visit. That too was odd, for the other farmers must have seen Arabella. After all, she did not come in the night or try to hide from anyone. Kristin's questions, it appeared, were just beginning.

*

Sawney and Tavan halted their horses next to each other on the top of the hill, and looked down on the glen and the village below. Sawney's guards spread out and were not far away, yet not close enough to hear. In spring, the view from there was exceptional, but just now the grass lands were still a little too brown. More rain would correct that problem soon enough.

Sawney looked up at the sky hoping for more rain, but it was still clear. At length he said, "We shall have to fight to get her out."

"I suspected as much."

"You did not believe Buchannan?"

"He does it quite well…lie, I mean, but he will not bring her back. Daughters are a possession and his pride will not let him."

"You have become wise, my son."

"Not wise enough. I should not have let her show herself."

"You did not know why he came."

"True."

"Do you love her?"

It was none of his father's business, so Tavan gave him the vaguest answer he could think of, "I do not know."

Sawney found those words encouraging, but just in case, he had to be careful not to make Tavan feel he had to defend her. "I have been remiss in not telling you about Arabella. You had not heard?"

"I was as surprised as Kristin."

"Then I tell you now. The people will talk and they will have much to say, most of which is unpleasant. Some believe Arabella killed her mother."

Tavan's mouth dropped. "Is it true?"

"I have always believed it, but no one kills without a reason. Whatever happened, I tend to think Arabella must have had just cause. Her mother was…" Sawney was not exactly certain how he should explain it.

"Go on, what was she?"

"Wanton."

"I see."

"A willing lass is shunned by the clan, therefore Murdina was forced to stay away except when she needed something. She kept to the forest mostly."

"You are saying Arabella was the same?"

"I have heard from some that she was. She too liked to wander in the forest."

"The same as Kristin, you mean." Tavan could not help but show his disgust.

"I do not deny that some believe it is in the blood."

"Do you believe it?"

"I do not know what to believe." Sawney could see Tavan was beginning to get defensive and hoped to avoid it. "I worry over what Samuel might do."

"As do I. I promised Kristin I would look after him. I also told one of the farmers what happened. They will see to him."

Sawney nodded and then looked away. He could remember every detail as though it were yesterday. "Samuel nearly went daft after

Arabella left him. He once said, there is no pain like it in the world and I am certain it is so. I could not bear it if your mother went to another lad's bed. I doubt I could ever understand it, but Samuel is a better lad than I...a far better lad than I."

Sawney's horse became restless and it took a moment to calm the stallion down. Then he pointed. "Look there, it begins already."

"Where, Father?"

"There. Do you see the lad walking down the glen? Now look at the lass who stands in her doorway watching him."

"What is wrong?"

"Arabella is dead. The lad goes off to grieve and his wife suspects."

"He loved Arabella too?"

"Why else would he walk away when the evening meal is almost upon us. He is a builder, not a hunter or a guard, and he has no excuse. He may pretend to look after his horse, that is, if he is wise. There are others who will be grateful to be a guard this night. I saw the same when Arabella's mother disappeared. It was weeks before the husbands and wives settled down. Some wives never did forgive completely."

"Was Arabella's mother that tempting?"

"I have heard she had a way about her. It is easy for a lad to confuse love with desire. Some lads marry wrongly because of it. I suspect once they marry the wrong lass, they are the ones most easily tempted by the lasses among us who are willing."

Tavan smiled. "You mean to warn me against a bad marriage?"

"If I can." He returned his son's smile and then watched the people in the glen for a while longer. "These hills are full of secrets. Some of Arabella's secrets will remain in the leaves, but I suspect we are in for a fortnight of more gossip than any of us desire to hear."

Both father and son were lost in thought for several minutes. Then Sawney began to speak again, "Buchannan brought forty with him. I put our lads in the woods on each side of the glen and just before the Buchannan entered, word came of many more in the trees behind our lads."

Tavan was surprised. "They had us trapped."

"Aye, many would have died if either you or I had thought to keep Buchannan from taking her. I am pleased you did not."

"She said she prayed no MacGreagor blood would be shed on her account. I believe that is why she went with him, that and because she wanted the adventure."

"Letting her go without a fight can be used to our advantage."

"How so?"

"Buchannan will see it as a weakness. We must be very careful not to let him think otherwise."

"What do you mean to do?"

"Have you any suggestions?"

Tavan thought hard about that. "They will be watching us. Perhaps we should give them something to see."

"Precisely what I was thinking."

*

Kristin loved riding and sometimes won races against the men during festivals. The thought that they were moving slower than was necessary for her sake, made her inwardly laugh at them. She might have suggested a faster pace, but there were plenty of trees and flowers to see along the way, and it was more fun just to let them believe she was too tender for a real ride. At last, Hendry's men stopped to rest near a pleasant pond where the horses could drink their fill. As soon as she slid down, she started into the trees.

"Kristin, you must not wander off," Hendry said.

She turned and smiled. "But I must."

She did not ask permission, which Hendry found a bit annoying, but she would learn. "Kristin is a bit willful, do you not agree?" he asked Michael.

"Aye." Standing not far from the pond, Michael waited until he could no longer see Kristin, untied his water flask and took several swallows. "She is very much like Arabella." It was the first time anyone had the courage to speak Arabella's name since her death and Michael held his breath. He expected Hendry to fly into a rage, but he did not. Perhaps having Kristin around would ease the tension in the village.

"Her likeness is a bit disturbing, is it not? Even the sound of her voice is like her mother's." Hendry took another long drink of wine from his flask and wiped his mouth. "I gave my pledge to bring her back in a fortnight, but I aim to keep her."

"How?"

"Laird MacGreagor said they do not force a lass to come or go. Therefore, I must make her agree to stay."

Michael considered that. "If she is as much like her mother as we think, keeping her will not be easy. How will you convince her?"

"I have thought of that. Where are Arabella's belongings?"

"We put them in the storehouse."

"Good, I shall give Kristin a gift each morning."

For hours, Michael wondered what he would say when Hendry began to question him. There were many rumors about Arabella, but over the years few were witless enough to tell Hendry what he clearly did not want to hear. Today Hendry's eyes had been opened and the moment of truth was upon him...unless Michael could think of a way out of it.

"Did you know she gave Kristin to the MacGreagor?"

"Nay, 'twas before my time. I did not know until the MacGreagors told us just now."

"I forget you are so young. Did you not hear tell of it from the elders though?"

Michael prayed he was just as accomplished at lying, as his laird. He knew better than to look away from Hendry's piercing eyes and forced himself not to. "Nary a word was spoken to me. 'Twas a long time ago."

Hendry considered that. "Seventeen years is a long time. I wonder how the MacGreagors managed to keep it a secret."

"I cannot guess, but we did not fail to keep our secret. They did not know of Arabella's death before we arrived."

"I am pleased to hear that. Well done, Michael." If Michael was lying, which Hendry decided he must be, he was very good at it. Hendry glanced around, saw that his men were quietly talking to one another, and wondered if he could trust any of them now. One or two who betrayed him could be done away with, but he could hardly kill them all.

Hendry tried to remember exactly what happened when Kristin was born. He was away that month complete and when he returned, Arabella said her labor began in the forest and she did not get home in time. The child did not draw breath, and she buried it so the animals would not eat it. Once she was able, she took the men to the grave to give the child a proper burial, but the animals had gotten to it. "She...buried the afterbirth," he muttered.

"What?" Michael asked.

Hendry ignored the question. "If a motherless child came to our village, everyone would know about it. The elders knew about Kristin, they must have."

"Was it not you who forbid us to speak to the MacGreagors? Why was that, I have never known."

"Arabella wished it. She said..." Another lie, he realized, another among how many - hundreds? It was enough to make a man daft.

"She said what?" His laird did not answer and Michael let it pass. If Hendry was resolved to seek revenge against the elders, they were in for a nasty time and there was little he could do about it. "Should I gather the elders when we get home?"

Hendry took another long swig of wine and then began to retie his flask. "Someday, but not just yet. I wish Kristin to find only happiness with us."

"Agreed." Michael remembered to breath and glanced toward the trees just in time to see Kristin coming back. He thought perhaps he has just survived the worst of it, but with Hendry, no one could be quite certain.

CHAPTER VI

From the top of the final hill, her view of the Buchannan village was all Kristin expected and more. The Buchannan glen was not as long or as wide, but trees had been cut down along the edges, leaving stumps for the clan to sit on if they wished. The trees were obviously used to build a tall fence around the village and each tree trunk had been sharpened to a point at the top, to dissuade enemies from climbing over. There appeared to be four guard towers, one at each corner of an imperfect square.

The village inside the fence was vast and not so very different from the one she grew up in. Yet the Keep had four floors and was twice the size. It was made of stone and looked much like she imagined a castle to look. The tall building had few windows, and none had fine English window panes, but that was to be expected.

As soon as they rode down the hill and into the glen, the people paused to look at her. It was far from a pleasant experience, for none of them smiled and a few openly looked shocked. Just in time, the huge double gates opened outward, Laird Buchannan's guards parted and Hendry led the way through still more people waiting inside. Kristin was expecting the reaction this time and when her father did not stop to introduce her, she tried to look straight ahead as though she didn't notice all the eyes watching her.

"Arabella be not dead," a woman loudly said.

Kristin halted her horse and searched the faces in the crowd until she found the one who said it. The woman's eyes were filled with venom. "I am not Arabella, I am Kristin." She glared at the woman for several long moments before she nudged her horse forward again.

"'Tis Arabella, right enough," the woman dared mutter.

Kristin ignored her, but wondered why her father pretended not to notice. Surely he heard the exchange, yet he let it pass. Some father, she thought. Then again, perhaps she had to get used to such things and he was not willing to defend her each time. That was just as well, she had no trouble defending herself on all other occasions.

Some in the clan seemed pleased to have their laird home, but no one offered to help her dismount. No matter, she swung her leg over, turned around and dropped to the ground, careful not to let her legs show. She only had a moment to grab her sack before a boy led her horse away. A set of heavy wooden doors opened and she gladly followed her father inside where the people could not gawk at her.

The great hall was enormous and lavishly decorated, with colorful tapestries of the quality a wealthy laird would be expected to have. Unhappily, it was unkempt and smelled of must. The smell was not overbearing, but it was apparent a good scrubbing was long overdue. Arabella was always clean when she came to visit and Kristin wondered how her mother could have lived in such a place.

Surprisingly, the vast room was void of people, but someone had apparently been there not long before. Tall candles in iron holders on the walls were lit, which was a good thing once the doors began to close off the sunlight. The room was lavish indeed, if one did not count the harsh and brutal looking weapons between the tapestries.

Long-handled axes with sharp teeth would be enough to frighten most enemies away. Some of the swords were so old they had begun to rust while others looked like new, with leather straps wrapped around handles to make them easier to grip.

An ordinary long table took up the middle of the room, just as it did in the MacGreagor great hall, but this one needed a good polishing. Kristin's attention was soon drawn to a very wide staircase that began at the far end of the room, and curved upward. She set her sack on the table and was eager to get a good look at the carved banister. Instead, she watched Hendry pour two goblets of wine and then accepted the one he held out to her.

"Kristin, this is your home now. You may do as you please in it, save burn it down." He smiled. "We must see that you have Buchannan colors to wear."

"While I am here."

"Indeed, while you are here."

She took a sip of her wine and found it pleasing. "Have I any brothers and sisters?"

"You had five brothers, but they all died."

"I am sorry to hear that. I was hoping…"

"The best I can do is to marry again and give you one or two by half."

"You wish to marry again so soon?"

"I do not wish it, but a laird needs a wife and I need more sons."

She shrugged. He seemed pleased with the idea and Kristin did not care one way or the other. "Then the place has no one but you?"

"And you."

"For a fortnight." Her eyes were adjusted to the scant light finally and she looked around the room again. Several small tables were placed along the wall and the room had two hearths, one at each end. "I did hear you lost two sons in your war with the MacGraw. I am saddened I did not know them. Did you lose many others?"

He was not accustomed to being questioned about his affairs, but he answered her anyway. "Aye, too many, but not as many as the MacGraw."

"I see. We have not seen a war ourselves in many years."

"Aye, well perhaps the MacGreagors have not found something worth fighting for."

"Or, most clans fear provoking us. We covet peace, but our lads are strong and well trained. We will not run from a fight."

Hendry did not like her preferring to the MacGreagors as 'we' as though she belonged to them still, but it was just another thing he would correct later.

Instead of asking more questions, Kristin took another sip, set her goblet down on the table and went to get a closer look at the banister. Slowly, she ran her fingers across the forward and backward swirls in the wood. "It is magnificent."

"I am happy you approve. I am so accustomed to seeing it, I forget to notice."

She turned to look at him once more. "Do the people not want to come in to see you? Sawney is always…"

"They will come soon enough and then you will complain there are too many. Come, I will show you where you will sleep."

*

The bedchamber Laird Buchannan took his daughter to on the second floor was in far worse shape than the great hall. It had no window at all, it was cluttered with soiled clothing strewn everywhere and the bed was unmade. Trunks were left open, table tops were cleared and it looked as though someone had torn up the place.

"Is this my mother's bedchamber?"

"Aye."

"Did she die in that bed?"

He looked at the stricken expression on his daughter's face and realized what she was thinking. "Perhaps another would do better."

"Have you one with a window? I am fond of fresh air."

He pulled the door closed behind her, led the way down the hall and up a second flight of stairs. At first, he could not remember which room had a window, opened one door, closed it and opened the next. Satisfied, he stood back and let her go in. "Perhaps this will do. 'Tis safer up here anyway."

This room had little in it, but at least it had a window. "Thank you. Where do you sleep?"

"Next to your mother's bedchamber."

"I see."

"I will send a lass to care for you."

"Oh I do not need…"

"You are my daughter and you will have the best I can offer. You need not lift a finger while you are here." He nodded and closed the door.

Kristin listened to him walk down the stairs, and then put her sack on the bed. This room had cob webs in the corners and had not been dusted or cleaned in a good while, but at least it was not cluttered with Arabella's belongings. Cautiously, she walked to the window and looked out. There wasn't much to see, just a few thatched roofs, the fence and some of the trees beyond.

The window was small, too small for a man to get in, but she could fit through it if she had to. It was always wise to plot one's escape, Samuel once said. She missed him already and one thing bothered her greatly…if she was not to lift a finger, what on earth was she supposed to do with her time?

The door abruptly opened, a woman walked in and tossed a Buchannan plaid on the bed. "I am Myra; I am to care for you."

There was no mistaking the hate in the woman's eyes, but Kristin tried to overlook it. "Thank you. I wonder if I might have a pail of water, some wash cloths and some soap."

"You wish to bathe in a pail?"

"Nay, I wish to clean the place. I will need a broom as well."

Myra stared at her in disbelief. Her light brown hair was uncombed, her skin was weather beaten and her clothes were not much cleaner than the ones in Arabella's room. "I do the cleaning."

"Then I will help you."

"Laird Buchannan will not approve."

"Then we will not tell him."

The woman stared at Kristin a moment more, shrugged and started to leave.

"Myra."

"Aye."

"You need not hate me for my mother's sake, she will never

know. I am not like her, I assure you, but I will not allow you to treat me unkindly."

"What will you do?"

"Request another to care for me."

Myra quickly looked away. She had seen Hendry's fits of rage often enough to know not to cross him, and a complaint from his daughter would likely do her in. It was doubtful she would ever like Arabella's daughter, but she pretended to like Arabella and she could do it again. "You are more like your mother than you know." She nodded and left the room.

As soon as she was gone, Kristin realized her mistake. She should not have threatened her; it was not the best way to make a friend, and right now she needed one. Still, she could not appear weak.

*

Myra did not come back. Kristin sat on the edge of her bed waiting, got bored with her thoughts about what she could do to the room to make it more lively and thrummed her fingers on the dusty blanket. She could hear men laughing and talking downstairs and was glad her father was occupied.

Frustrated, Kristin finally opened the door and went out. She boldly walked down the stairs, then the hall and was about to descend the bottom stairs when she stopped. Myra was sitting in the lap of a man, drinking and laughing right along with the rest of them. Kristin contemplated what to do for a moment and then decided to ignore her. Trying not to draw attention to herself, she slipped down the stairs, walked around the gathering and was nearly out the door when her father shouted.

"Arabella, where are you going?"

The room went deadly quiet.

Enraged, Kristin clenched her fists, slowly turned around and glared with a glare as fierce as any had seen on her father's face. "My name is Kristin and I shall go wherever I like!" She started to turn back around, spotted a goblet on the table near Myra, picked it up and dumped the red liquid in the woman's lap. She never said a word, but when a shocked Myra's eyes met hers, Kristin's message was loud and clear. She ignored the other people, opened the door and slammed it behind her.

Every eye turned on Hendry. The tension was thick as they waited to see what their laird would do. Finally, Michael said, "If I doubted it before, I doubt it no longer. She *is* your daughter."

From the back, she looked so much like his dead wife, even Hendry was taken aback by his mistake. "And Arabella's."

One of the men looped a lazy arm over Michael's shoulders and grinned. "God help us now." It was enough to make everyone laugh and soon they resumed the evening's merriment.

Hendry sat back, took a swallow of wine, set his goblet down and listened to them for a little while. They admired his daughter for standing up to him. He could hear it in the things they did not say. In the beginning, he did not allow Arabella to show her true nature and perhaps that had been a mistake. He was young and thought he would appear weak if he could not control his wife. Arabella had her good points. She could be quite entertaining when she wanted to be. Yet when she was not there, the men mocked her and he let them get away with it.

They did not mock Kristin and he saw it as a very good thing. The war with the MacGraw did not go as well as he hoped. His men fought, but they had no stomach for it and nearly lost. Now he intended to fight the MacGreagors if he had to, to keep his daughter, and it would be to his advantage if they admired and liked her enough to fight for her.

"Michael, go with her," Hendry said finally.

"Me, why me?"

"Because she knows you. Be gone with you and do not come back without her."

Michael frowned and slowly got up. He was second in command, not a nursemaid. Let the women go with the women, just as they always had. Still, there was nothing he could do about it, so he begrudgingly walked out the door.

Myra was relieved no one seemed to notice when she left the lap of her husband to go find a dry skirt. Hendry did not ask why Kristin did that, and she could not guess what she would have said if he did. Had it been Arabella, the two women would have had a row right then and there, and given the clan something to talk about the next day, but Kristin's sort of silent anger was something new.

*

Kristin was so furious, she marched out of the courtyard and out of the wooden gates so fast, Michael had to quicken his pace to catch up with her. She went into the forest at the same place her mother always did and for a moment, Michael thought perhaps she *was* Arabella come back from the dead. He dismissed that thought and ignored all the people watching them. It was several minutes before she stopped, drew in a deep breath and turned around.

"Why do you follow me?"

He did not think she knew he was there. "Your father commanded it."

"I see." She bent down, examined and then picked three flowers in full bloom. She moved to another bush with blooms of a darker shade of pink, and did the same. When she glanced at him, he had his hands clasped behind his back watching her. "Why did you go to war with the MacGraw?"

"I cannot say."

"You cannot or you will not?"

"I will not."

She picked two more flowers and walked farther into the forest. "Are you married?"

"Aye."

"Children?"

"Aye, a son."

She turned to look him in the eye. "Do you love her?"

He wasn't too keen on answering a question as personal as that, but decided it wouldn't hurt. "She loves me. I do not know why, but if she does, then the least I can do is love her back." His remark made Kristin smile and he was glad. Her father did not yet act protective, but if that changed, Michael did not want to be accused of upsetting her.

"Does she keep your cottage clean?"

"Aye, some days it is too clean. She fills my goblet, I take a drink and when I reach for it again, she has put it away."

"My other father is the same. He prefers our cottage to be very clean. 'Tis why I was surprised to see how my mother lived."

"She was…" He almost forgot himself and stopped.

"Go on, I am listening."

He quickly glanced around to be certain they were safe. "How many flowers do you need, lass?"

She stopped and looked up at him. "How many will it take to make Hendry's keep smell pleasant?"

Michael nodded his understanding. "I will tell your father you wish it cleaned. The lasses will do it for you."

"I do not want to bother them, I can do it."

"All of it? It would take a year at least."

"I will have little else to do."

Despite himself, he was beginning to like her. First she stood up to her father, and now she cared that the woman did not have to take on more chores. Indeed, he was starting to like her a lot in spite of himself. "Perhaps you should let the lasses help. They want to know all about you, they will hound us for every detail and they will make the lads daft."

"Do you a good turn then? Perhaps I should, but do not force them. Let only those who want, come to help me."

"And if none come?"

She swatted a fly away from her face. "Then I will clean it myself…as much as I can in a fortnight."

He wished she had not reminded him of that. In a fortnight, there would be hell to pay when they didn't take her back.

*

It was nearly time for the evening meal when Tavan and Sawney rode back into the glen, dismounted and let two boys take their horses to the stables. Sawney ignored the inquiring eyes of those remaining outside and went home, but Tavan wanted a moment alone before he had to face his family's questions. The one place most people would not disturb someone was in the graveyard.

He stared at his grandfather's tall headstone and wished Justin was alive to advise him. He never knew his grandfather, but many said he was wise beyond his years. Tavan replayed the events of the days in his mind, to see if he could have done something differently, but he could think of nothing. Laird Buchannan meant to have his daughter one way or another and only time would tell if they managed to avoid a war, or just postpone it.

He was worried about her. The MacGreagors honored women, but other clansmen saw them as possessions to do with as they wished. Surely Samuel taught her how to kill a man if need be, but he could not be certain she could manage it on her own, no matter how much she believed in her own abilities. A woman simply was not as strong as a man.

Tavan glanced up at the sky and then turned around and faced the village. It would be dark in another hour and there was little he could do to help Kristin now. He was still not ready to answer all the questions, but he decided he might as well get it over with and began to walk to the Keep.

*

Word spread quickly and by the time Michael and Kristin returned, everyone knew Kristin was not afraid to stand up to her father. They also knew Laird Buchannan had not chastised her for it, and wondered just how long that would last. Nevertheless, when she walked back through the village, two women actually nodded and Kristin was delighted. Maybe it wasn't going to be so bad there after all.

Once inside, she ignored the men and went to each room on the bottom floor of his large keep looking for just one thing -- a vase to put her flowers in. She found a large kitchen, with three women in it preparing the evening meal, but she said nothing and neither did they. She was hungry and decided not to bother them.

She climbed the stairs, hoping to find something in her mother's bedchamber and went there first. It was not a pleasant place to be, so she quickly glanced around and then closed the door. The next bedchamber belonged to her father and she dared not look in there. She opened the door to three more rooms, found nothing useful and then sighed. The flowers would wilt soon, but perhaps they would keep for one night.

When she climbed the next flight of stairs and opened the door to her bedchamber, the room was spotless. The cobwebs were gone, the dusty blankets had been shaken and the floor swept. A bowl of fresh water sat on a table near the window, and although it was for washing, she happily began to set the flowers in it one by one. Perhaps she and Myra could become friends.

She finished setting the flowers in the bowl, found her sack in a chair, opened it and withdrew the carved horse Tavan had given her. She looked around, decided it would look best on a table near her bed and carefully set it there. Then she stood back and admired it. It was a comfort to have something of him with her.

*

As soon as Tavan entered the MacGreagor great hall, all eyes turned in his direction and everyone stopped talking. He nodded to his mother and then looked at his father. "What have you told them?"

"Only that Kristin went willingly and Laird Buchannan will return her in a fortnight."

"And?"

"And…that you were there."

Tavan rolled his eyes. "Father, could you not lie just once? Now their questions will be endless. They will tell others and I'll not have a moment's peace in a year, at least."

"Very well," Sawney said, "Tavan was *not* there." He got the laughter he hoped for. "Sit everyone."

The serving women brought in large bowls of food and the family took their usual seats at the table. It had been a trying day, the food smelled wonderful, and they were all hungry.

The family did indeed have many questions, but it took a while before Colina was brave enough to ask, "What truly happened, Father?"

"As I said before, Arabella confessed before she died, although Laird Buchannan was not certain she meant to. He came to get Kristin and she went willingly."

"She went to keep the MacGreagors from having to fight for her," Tavan added.

Callum eyed his brother? "You talked to her?"

"Aye, we were in the forest picking berries when we saw father and Laird Buchannan coming."

"And," Graw asked.

"And nothing," Tavan answered.

"There must be more to tell than that. Did you give Kristin your pledge?" asked Patrick.

Tavan slowly chewed his bite of beef and swallowed. "Aye."

Every mouth dropped, even Sawney's.

Bardie's eyes were wide. "You pledged to marry her?"

"Nay, I pledged to care for Samuel while she is away." The sigh of relief from each member of his family made him laugh. "As I recall, last night you wished to marry me off...and quickly. What has changed?"

Mackinzie put her hand over her son's. "'Tis only that a betrothal to one who might not come back is..."

"Do not fret, Mother, I know what you are saying. I will abide by her decision if she chooses to stay. I shall have no choice."

"How will we know if she wishes to come home, but Laird Buchannan will not let her?" Colina asked.

"Kristin promised to send word if we are needed."

"Oh." Colina lost interest in that subject soon enough and turned to Sawney. "Father, who was Arabella, truly?"

Sawney chose his words carefully. "She was a lass who erred in many ways."

"They say she was wanton." said Colina.

"Who says it?" Tavan asked.

"Everyone. They say Kristin will be just like her, 'tis in her blood."

Sawney watched to see how Tavan was going to react. He

expected someone to say it, but not his eldest daughter and not quite so soon. Tavan did not seem disturbed, so he turned back to Colina. "What do you say she will be? You know Kristin as well as any of us."

Colina considered his question for a moment. "Well, she is a bit quiet. She comes sometimes to watch the courting, but she never comes inside the courtyard where the lads can approach her. She is not yet ready to marry, perhaps, but I see no harm in letting a lad approach."

It was the perfect opportunity for Tavan to change the subject. "Have you chosen a husband yet, sister?"

"You know I have not, why do you ask?"

"Some say you will choose either Parlan or Alec."

"Parlan? He prefers Senga and everyone knows it…save Senga. Why he does not approach her is beyond me."

"And Alec? Do you prefer him?" Tavan asked.

Colina wrinkled her brow. "Do you think he would make a good husband?"

"If he loves you, he will be the bravest lad I know," said Patrick. As he expected, she let her spoon drop into her bowl and defiantly put her hands on her hips.

Tavan smiled at his little sister. "I like Alec; he is a good lad and a brave fighter."

"Then I will consider him." She picked up her spoon again and took another bite of stew.

Everyone seemed to be watching Tavan, especially his brothers and he was beginning to get annoyed. "Arabella had two sons, both lost in war, I hear."

"Nay," said Mackinzie. "She had five, all lost."

"Five sons?" asked Sawney. "All dead before their father? I cannot imagine that pain."

"God's punishment, perhaps," said Mackinzie. "I wonder that Arabella had no other daughters?"

"Fib had five sons in a row, 'tis not that uncommon," said Callum.

"Fib has a daughter now," said Mackinzie.

"True," Callum admitted.

Tavan had forgotten all about the switched babies and still he said nothing. Right before his eyes, on this very day, he had seen what telling secrets could do to a family. He vowed that one would never leave his lips.

Mackinzie sighed. "If Arabella was wanton, who is to say who fathered her sons?"

"Wife, 'tis far too late now. Arabella and all her sons are dead."

"I know, but you must admit it is intriguing."

Patrick finished eating, pushed his bowl away and folded his arms. "Mother, you best not say it around others. There are too many wives who fear their husbands have..."

Mackinzie gasped. "MacGreagors would never do such a thing."

"Why not?" Colina asked, "Arabella was a MacGreagor and we know of at least two lads she bedded."

Sawney also pushed his bowl away and began to rub his brow. He did not think Bardie should hear such things, but if she had questions, he was happy to let her ask...her mother. The problem of Arabella was far worse than that, and he could only pray tempers would not rise to the point of telling all.

"Father," Colina asked, "Who was Ainsley?"

Sawney abruptly stopped rubbing his brow. "Where did you hear that name?"

"Sharla's mother said he died. She started to tell us what happened, but changed her mind. Now she will not speak of it."

So it had begun already, Sawney thought. "When you hear such things, come ask me for the truth. Memories become clouded, rumors begin, and the truth some tell is not the truth at all. Promise you will ask me."

"I promise, Father, but what happened to Ainsley?"

Sawney took a deep breath. "Someone set him on fire." Sawney could still hear the man's screams and had to close his eyes to push the memory away. When he opened them again, every member of his family was staring at him.

"Did Arabella do it?" Patrick asked.

"I do not know. Some say she did, but there was no proof."

Mackinzie drew in a forgotten breath. "There is nothing I fear more than fire."

"Which reminds me," said Tavan, 'tis my night to keep watch." He nodded to his father, got up and started up the stairs. Three flights, one step at a time gave him a few moments to gather his wits before he joined the other men. Sawney tried to warn him, but to hear his sister say Kristin would be wanton like her mother, was harder than he expected. He had an urge to put his arms around Kristin and protect her somehow. He could still see her smiling and picking flowers without a care in the world. Now, no one would ever be able to give her that peaceful world back...not even him.

The night was even less peaceful for Sawney. For a man who rarely had nightmares, the mention of Ainsley made Sawney dream in vivid colors of red and yellow. It was true, no one saw who set him on fire, but once Ainsley ran out of the forest into the glen, his screams and his horror was there for everyone to see. Mothers hurried children away, while the men ran for buckets of water. It was too late. Ainsley's kilt and shirt were fully engulfed and once he fell to the ground, Sawney prayed a quick death would end the man's torment. At last, the fire was doused, yet it was several minutes before Ainsley breathed his last.

Fire meant certain death to them all, and the men hurried into the forest to make certain it would not spread. It was then Sawney saw it for himself and quickly picked up -- a half-used candle tossed in a bush. Thankfully, the forest fire was put out before it could get a good start and no harm came to anyone else. Still, he had a murder on his hands and many questions to ask. All these years later, he still had no answers.

It was easy to blame Arabella since everyone was still upset over her leaving Samuel, but why Arabella would have done it had no answer either. It was just one of those secrets no one was willing to tell.

CHAPTER VII

The men in the Buchannan great hall were loud and very drunk by the time Kristin stopped listening to their stories. She sat at the opposite end of the table from her father, who slurred his words and twice let his head fall to the table. Each time brought insulting laughter from the others. The women were just as bad, flirting with every man there, husband or not, and drinking just as much as the men.

She noticed Michael watching her a time or two, but tried not to pay particular attention to him. He seemed the only one still sober, which she suspected was intentional, since he was second in command and his sharp mind would be needed if they came under attack.

Half of the stories they told were nonsense, yet the people listened and laughed or cheered at the end, as if hearing it for the first time. It made her feel a little ill at ease, for she had not guessed the people were simple minded.

Even after she went up to bed, sleep was not easy to come by with all the noise, and she sorely wished she were on the fourth floor instead of the third. She thought about Tavan too and the peaceful time before Hendry came. How she longed to get that hour or two back. She missed Tavan's comforting smile, his strong arms around her and wondered how she could have let those precious moments slip by nearly unnoticed. She closed her eyes and imagined herself back in his safe arms. It helped some, but it didn't blot out the noise two floors below.

Late in the night, she heard the men bring her father up the stairs and put him to bed. At last, it got quiet and she fell asleep.

*

An early riser all her life, Kristin was awake before the roosters began to crow, got dressed and then brushed and braided her hair. The Buchannan plaid Myra gave her was not in good condition, but Kristin guessed she could find something better in her mother's bedchamber later in the day. It was still odd to think of Arabella as her mother, but what she found stranger still, was the lack of her name being mentioned the night before. Not one story included Arabella and even Kristin's father had not brought her up. Perhaps Hendry forbade them to mention her.

She suspected her father would not feel at all well when he awoke and therefore, quietly opened her door and went down. To her surprise, Michael sat at the long table with seven women, each eating a hearty morning meal.

When he spotted her, he motioned for her to come, waited for Kristin to take a seat and then passed a bowl of potage down to her.

"Thank you," she whispered.

Michael laughed, "A thousand thundering horses cannot wake your father most mornings. You'll have plenty of time to do your cleaning downstairs before he rises, and these lasses want to help."

He introduced them one at a time, and Kristin repeated their names so she could remember them. Myra was among them and she took special care to smile, so the woman would know she harbored no resentment. Then she began to quietly eat. She noticed the silence, looked up and realized they were watching her instead of eating. "You may ask me anything you wish."

"Anything?" Myra asked.

"Aye, what do you wish to know?"

"Is it true a MacGreagor is put to death if he forces a lass?"

"Aye, 'tis an edict from long ago. A lad who harms a lass or a child shall be put to death."

"Even if he only forces..."

"Forcing a lass harms her just as much as striking her." Kristin took another bite of oats, chewed and swallowed. "A lad does not know if a lass is with child, not until her stomach swells. Forcing her might harm another lad's son. For that, he must surely die."

Michael wasn't certain he liked the women hearing this, for there was no such law among the Buchannan. "What if a lass does wrong?"

"Then she is brought before our laird and her crime judged. Now, if a child lies or steals, they are made to clean up after the horses for a fortnight." She grinned as each turned up their noses at the thought.

"But if a lass is judged guilty, what shall her punishment be?" Michael asked.

"Tis never the same." Kristin looked at the worried expressions on each of their faces, and then slowly smiled. "A lass who does not know what the punishment will be, takes care not to raise Sawney's ire. On the other hand, a wife who harms her husband or her children shall be banished. A lass is not put to death for the possible unborn child's sake."

Michael heard rumors of the edict, but no one had been able to explain so thoroughly before. "'Tis reasonable."

"We think so. Now," she continued looking at the women, "are you willing to help me clean the place?" She was pleased when each of them nodded. Together they finished eating, and decided the great hall was a good place to start before the men cluttered it up again.

*

Michael came three times to see how Kristin's cleaning was coming along, and nodded his approval after each inspection. Then on the fourth visit, he brought his wife. "My Mary picked flowers for you."

Mary was a small woman with a round face and a sweet smile. It was easy to see why Michael loved her, and as he said, a little difficult to see why she would love an ox of a man like him. "I am grateful, Mary. I do not have time today to pick them and I do so love fresh flowers." Mary curtsied, which Kristin found endearing, and then hurried out the door.

"She's a bit shy at first, but once she gets on, you'll not likely shut her up," said Michael.

"She is very pleasing."

"Aye, she is." He smiled and then went out the door as well.

Kristin set the basket of flowers on a clean table and puffed her cheeks. It appeared she had Michael's acceptance and it was a giant step in the right direction, if she wanted her two week stay to be pleasant.

*

After a night of watching for fires from the third-floor windows of the MacGreagor keep, Tavan was more than ready to go to the Carley cottage and sleep. He imagined every possible horror Kristin might have endured during the night, and had to repeatedly remind himself her father would not let anything happen. If Laird Buchannan wanted her bad enough to fight the MacGreagors, he would protect her.

The night sky was just beginning to lighten by the time he went outside. Something in the long shadows suddenly moved and he quickly drew his sword. "Who goes there?"

"'T-t-tis o-o-nly I," said the voice of a woman. She approached with caution and smiled.

He put his sword away and returned her smile. At just a bit over four feet, Sile was the smallest of all the women, even wrapped up as she was, in two plaids to ward off the cold. "Sile, why are you out at this time of morning?"

Most did not ignore Sile on purpose, but she spoke with a stammer and it took patience to wait for her answer. "I...h-h-hunger."

"You have nothing to eat in your cottage?"

"N-n-ay."

"Come, I will go with you."

She was happy for his company, skillfully led the way to the storehouse in the dim light, and tried to open the door. Unfortunately, it was too heavy for her, which it always was. Unless she came for food at a time when someone was there to help, she had to do without.

"I will do it," said Tavan. He took the sack she handed him, went inside and opened the strings to the first large sack he came to. He found the ladle inside, dipped the oats and filled her bag completely full. Just as he was about to come out, he heard another voice.

"Sile, what is wrong?" Gordon asked.

"She is hungry," Tavan said, as he walked out and pulled the door closed behind him. "Sile, why did you not tell someone the door is too heavy for you?"

"I...d-d-do not...w-w-want...t-t-to b-b-bother...t-t-them."

Tavan was not pleased. "We cannot have you go without food. From now on, you are to come to me when you need help."

She smiled. For a moment she feared Tavan would make Gordon help her, and of all the men in the clan, Gordon was her least favorite. "T-t-thank...y-y-ou." It was with good cause she disliked Gordon and he knew it too. Most of the time, he was as pleased to stay clear of her as she was to avoid him. It was no surprise to her that Gordon was the first to claim Arabella was wanton - no surprise at all, for he had been saying it for years.

"Come, I will take you home," said Tavan.

Sile turned and led the way down the path to her cottage. Once there, she took the sack from Tavan, nodded her appreciation and went inside. She set her bag on the table, dipped her hand in, withdrew a handful, and quickly picked out the small twigs. Then she hungrily began to eat the dry oats.

Usually, she simply waited until someone came who could open the door. This day however, she knew her red eyes would beg questions from the others -- questions she did not want to answer. How could she tell them she mourned the death of someone they all found despicable?

*

The noon meal was upon them by the time Tavan woke up. He dreamed an odd sort of dream, most of which he could not remember later. It was not about Kristin, but of a very sad Sile. For years, Sile helped his mother and often cared for him, his brothers and sisters. That was before she became too old to climb two flights of stairs without a great deal of pain. It was true, Sile stuttered and it required patience to listen to her, that is, until she got mad. When that happened, the triplets knew they best get out of her way, and fast. Yet, no woman save their mother, had more love for them, and Tavan felt bad for not knowing the door was too heavy for her.

A long-time widow, Sile still came to the great hall to visit occasionally, normally at meal time and was always invited to join them. Her hips might have pained her later in life, but there was never anything wrong with her appetite. The triplets often claimed she devoured more than the three of them combined.

Once Tavan was dressed, he left the cottage and expected to spend the rest of the day helping his father make plans for getting Kristin back. There were spies to send and maps to draw of the Buchannan village. They already knew the village was enclosed by a tall fence that would have to be breached somehow, but how? Tavan's thoughts were of the coming war when he walked up the path and nearly ran into Sharla.

"Oh there you are. Are you unwell?" she asked.

"Do I look unwell?" he asked.

"Nay, but I thought seeing our dear Kristin cruelly carried off like that, might have made you a bit upset."

Wherever Sharla was, Jenae seemed to be close by, and when he spotted her sitting on a tree stump, she rolled her eyes. Apparently, she was thinking the same thing -- Sharla was prodding him for information, which would soon turn to gossip and come back to haunt him. He looked deep into Sharla's eyes and wrinkled his brow. "'Tis you who are unwell, I see."

"Me? How so?"

"I have seen far more light in your eyes than I see now. Have you not eaten? Perhaps if you did, your skin would not look so pale. Forgive me, father is waiting." He walked around her, winked at Jenae and went on his way.

Truly upset, Sharla caught her breath, covered her mouth with her hand and hurried back inside her cottage.

Jenae dared not giggle or even smile. After all, her dearest friend was very ill indeed, or thought she might be, and with any luck, would take to her bed. It would be Jenae's duty to look in on her and perhaps, just perhaps, she might agree with Tavan...thereby keeping Sharla in bed the whole day. An entire afternoon without Sharla opened up a lot of possibilities. If Tavan had not noticed Jenae before, he had now and the two of them shared a conspiracy of sorts. What fun they could have and it just might help her win the wager.

Unfortunately Tavan spent the rest of the day in the Keep, and although she watched for him, he did not come to walk in the glen. She guessed he had gone back to his carving.

*

For most of the afternoon, once Hendry was awake that is, Kristin's father sat near the hearth with his aching head in his hands. Occasionally, someone entered and asked for directions on one issue or another, but for the most part they left him be.

Once, while she was washing the banister, she caught him staring at her. She assumed his head was not yet clear and he was seeing

Arabella instead. It would take a while, she guessed, for him to be certain she was his daughter, not his wife. Then, as abruptly as any man could, he stood up, walked to a trunk, opened it and reached inside. He pulled out a cloth sack, widened the drawstrings, and withdrew a jeweled goblet.

"'Twas your mother's," he said, as he handed it to her.

She took the appropriate amount of time to admire it and smiled. "'Tis beautiful and I thank you."

He said nothing more, only went back to his chair and sat down. Perhaps there was nothing more to say. Kristin might have cherished it better had Arabella been the aunt she loved, instead of the mother who deserted her. Nevertheless, it was a pleasing gift and something her father wanted her to have. Now, however, she wondered what she would do with it once she got home. Hide it perhaps, for it would be a reminder to Samuel of the pain he suffered. She left her cleaning, put the goblet in her bedchamber and by the time she returned, Hendry was gone.

*

After an exhausting day of hard work, Kristin was ready for a filling evening meal and a good night's sleep. It was not to be. Once more, the rowdy men gathered in the great hall, and paid far more attention to the wine and women, than to the cleanliness of the room.

The evening meal of beef stew tasted very good and she remembered to mention it to her father at the other end of the table, although she was forced to shout above the others. He hardly touched his meal, she noticed, and was wasting no time drinking his headache away.

All at once, she felt a hand on her knee and when she turned to look at the man seated next to her, she found his sickening grin disgusting. Before he could react, she stood up, drew her dagger and put the tip in the hollow of his neck. "If you dare touch me again, I shall find you in the night and cut you ear to ear."

The man stared into her determined eyes, but he was not as afraid of her as he was her father, and when she withdrew her dagger, he turned to look at his laird.

Hendry was glaring, but he did not stand or draw his sword. "Be gone with you, all of you. I will speak to my daughter alone." Obediently, they hurried out, all but Michael. "Have you something to say, Michael?"

"Aye, you look like hell." He nodded to Kristin and walked out the door. It had been weeks since he shared a meal with his family and he was glad to have the chance, but instead of starting down the path to his cottage, he paused to consider if Kristin could handle Hendry, should he become enraged. He satisfied himself that she could and went on his way.

Once all of them were gone and the room was quiet, Kristin picked up her bowl and went to sit beside her father. She ate in silence for a few minutes more and then could not help but say, "Your drunkenness makes you weak. Can you not eat?"

He looked long into her eyes. She pleased him very much and he wondered for a moment if he could truly trust her. She must care for him or she would not have said it. "A laird has many enemies. Padrig, the lad you threatened to kill, is one of them."

Hendry was not as drunk as she thought, she decided. "He is a pig."

"Aye, he is. Do not trust any lad." Hendry picked up his spoon and began to eat. "I was grateful for a reason to send them away."

Hendry's slurred speech vanished, his eyes looked brighter than they should have, and she guessed he was drinking water instead of wine. "And Michael? Do you trust him?"

"A laird dare not trust any lad completely, but Michael has always stood with me. I shall be called out soon."

"I would not like losing you so soon."

It was probably the most sincere and loving thing anyone had ever said to him and it warmed his heart. "I shall not like losing you either."

"I can come to you often. We do not live so very far apart...an afternoon ride is all."

"Aye, 'tis an easy ride." He ate a couple more bites before he spoke again, "You were not pleased with the goblet."

"It is very fanciful, but I know not what to do with such wealth. May I keep it here, where I can see it when I come to visit?"

"You may." Hendry was disappointed. While wealth kept Arabella happy, his daughter apparently did not find much joy in it. Convincing her to stay just got a little harder, he imagined, now that she thought to solve the problem by visiting often. He was beginning to love her a little, but it was far more important for her to love him enough to obey when the time came. Already there were rumors that the MacGraw wanted revenge and since Laird MacGraw was still unmarried, the pleasing Kristin might be the best way to avoid another war.

On the other hand, if he married her off, he would raise the ire of the MacGreagors. In less than three days, he managed to discover two warriors who wanted to challenge his position, and boxed himself in between a clan on either side of his land, who would not hesitate to attack if provoked. Hopefully, they would not join forces against him. It was the way of clans…war, revenge and another war, spread down through the generations until no one remembered what the original dispute was about. Such was the war with the MacGraw.

When he heard the door begin to open, he suddenly looked up, "What is it?"

"MacGreagors," Michael announced, quickly walking toward them.

"Where?" Kristin asked.

"Spies in the woods. We were fortunate to see them before they got any closer."

Kristin grinned. "You mean they *let* you see them. I assure you, they are very good at hiding even in sparse woods. Some are even better than me."

"Why have they *let* us see them?" Michael asked.

"To tell me they are close should I need them. I will go out so they can know I am well." She stood up and walked out the door. The days were not yet shortened, it was still light out and Kristin simply stood in the courtyard and slowly turned around so they could see her from all angles. Curious, she also carefully checked her surroundings to see from where she could be seen. There were the open gates, of course, and the hill she was on when she first saw the village, but other than that, the high fence kept an enemy from seeing much. A few minutes later, she went back inside. If the Buchannans in the courtyard thought her a little daft, they did not mention it.

*

The next morning, Sharla was the picture of health…at least she thought she was. She stood in front of the small mirror on her wall, pulled her lower eyelids down and decided the light was back in her eyes. Whatever plagued her the day before was gone. She checked to make certain her hair was neatly braided and then went out to find Jenae.

It was probably too early to see much of Tavan. He normally shared his morning meal with his family and after, he would talk to the men about whatever the men talked about that early in the morning. She found the whole process dreary, but she best learn to love it if she hoped to be Tavan's wife.

She did not expect to see what she saw next, and it instantly irked her. Jenae and Tavan were on horseback, riding off together toward the gardens. What could they possibly be doing? Jenae tricked him somehow; Sharla was certain of it. For a moment, she considered riding after them, but that would be too obvious. She was not at all pleased and narrowed her eyes.

*

"You need not go with me, Tavan," Jenae said as she followed him on the narrow path. "I have gone alone many times before without getting lost."

Tavan smiled and turned to look back at her. "I go to see Samuel this morning."

"I see, I think of him often too. I know how much he loves Kristin and how upset he must be."

"You know Kristin well?"

"As well as any, I suppose. My aunt and uncle work the land and I see her sometimes. She is always pleasant to me. In fact, I have never found her to be unpleasant."

"I do not know her well at all."

"I am not surprised. She favors being alone, I think. You should see her fight."

"Fight?"

"Aye, she fights as well as any lad I have seen. Her father taught her…of course, now everyone knows he is not her father."

"Did you know before Laird Buchannan came to get her?"

"Farmers keep even fewer secrets from each other than villagers do. I have seen Arabella as well. I was charged not to tell, so I did not."

"You come to this glen often?"

"I especially come in spring when the calves and lambs are born. They tell me the cows and sheep were once kept in our glen, where watching the little ones was much easier. We can still watch the colts in the glen, but that is all. I suppose it cannot be helped, the herds are too large now."

"We are too large as well."

"True, but I would not mind a few in the glen. I love watching them grow and play when they are small. The calves have all that hair on their heads and I sometimes laugh at how they have to peek through it to find their mothers."

When the path was wide enough, he slowed his horse until she caught up. "I would find the hair annoying."

"So would I. I am most happy to have hands instead of hooves." Jenae waved to a man working at the other end of the gardens. "Looks like it will rain again and will we not all be glad?" Without saying goodbye, she turned down a different path and rode away.

"Aye," he said too softly for her to hear. He liked Jenae; she was easy to talk to and seemed pleased with the world. He also liked that she kept Arabella's secret and did not ask him any questions about Kristin. Compared to Sharla, Jenae was a breath of fresh air.

Tavan was relieved to see Samuel on his horse, hard at work herding the cattle. The clouds were becoming a darker gray and soon all of them would don their leather cloaks or head for cover. Tavan slowly wove his horse through the cattle until he came face to face with Samuel.

"Kristin asked you to care for me?" Samuel asked.

"Aye," Tavan answered. "Come what may, she loves you first."

Samuel believed that, but it eased his mind to hear someone else say it. "I am well, Tavan, no need to fret."

"Good. I have also come to ask a favor. Sile cannot open the door to the storage shed and has been going without. Might you bring her some fresh vegetables when you came to the village next?"

Samuel eyed him suspiciously. "Your father wishes to marry me off, does he?"

Tavan chuckled. "Nay he does not yet know about Sile, but I suspect he will try to marry you off soon enough."

"One wife be more than enough for this old lad."

"I can see why." Tavan turned his horse around. "You will see to Sile?"

"Aye, I will see she has plenty to eat." Samuel returned Tavan's nod and watched him weave his way back through the cattle. He didn't much care for Sile, but she was a MacGreagor and he would do what he could for her.

*

Kristin had a lot to think about. There was intrigue afoot and watching her father try to draw his enemies out, if indeed that was what he was up to, was fascinating. Nevertheless, the night before, she guessed no one in the world needed a good night's sleep more than she did.

Up at her usual time, she found only one woman downstairs, the one who came to make the morning meal. Not long after Kristin sat down at the table, eighteen more came to help with the cleaning. They introduced themselves, assured her they had already eaten and sat in various places around the room to wait.

"Why did you stand in the courtyard alone?" one asked.

Kristin was surprised they did not already know and wondered if she should say, but then, the moment called for honesty and her father did not command her not to tell. "MacGreagors came and I wished them to see that I am well. They are gone home now." She took another bite of the cooked barley with sweet cream and swallowed. "Now I have a question. What was my mother like?"

"Proud," one of the women quickly answered.

"Proud?" She did not know what she expected them to say, but proud would not have been her first guess. "Did she have many friends?" Her second question was met with complete silence, which made her consider a different approach. "I did not know she was my mother, I believed she was my aunt. She came to see us…oh twice or three times a year. I did not know her well, but I did not think her proud."

Myra exchanged glances with another woman before she asked, "She came to see you?"

"Aye." Kristin went back to her meal. She hoped if they asked questions instead, she might learn more, but it didn't work. "Later, will you take me to see her grave? While I did not know she was my mother, she was a beloved aunt."

Myra wrinkled her brow. "I did not think Arabella was beloved to anyone."

"Not even to Hendry?"

The woman seated next to Myra rolled her eyes. "He loved her, to be sure. He must have or he would not have…"

Myra gave the woman a harsh look. "Say no more."

"Why not?" Kristin asked.

"'Tis not a happy memory and we do not speak of it," Myra explained.

Kristin wanted to know every detail, but doubted anyone would tell her now that Myra hushed them. "If you like, I will clean Arabella's bedchamber alone." When several of the women nodded, Kristin smiled.

It did not take long for that many women to clean the upstairs portion of the Buchannan keep and just as she promised, Kristin was prepared to clean her mother's bedchamber by herself. However, when she gathered Arabella clothing and suggested they burn them, it delighted the women so, they were happy to help her clean that room as well. The only room left unclean was Hendry's bedchamber.

It was late afternoon when Kristin decided to take a walk to see what the rest of the village was like. She paused to watch three children play an unfamiliar hopping game with stones in the courtyard. When an article of clothing fell out of a woman's basket, she happily picked it up and handed it to her. Her kindness was rewarded with a nod. It was apparent the women did not yet know what to make of her. Some quickly got out of her way; others simply ignored her.

Michael's wife had just finished baking bread when she spotted Kristin coming down the path, stepped outside and smiled. "You are well this day?"

"Aye, very well."

"Come, the bread is best when it is hot and I have butter."

"Thank you, Mary." Michael's cottage was ordinary with two small rooms, a table and chairs, and beds enough for their little family. The toddler waited for Kristin to sit and then begged to be in her lap. Kristin gladly lifted him up and turned him around so he could face forward.

"He will eat your bread if you let him."

"I will not mind." She waited for Mary to break off a chunk and then spread butter on it with the back of a spoon. It smelled wonderful and she was tempted to eat it all, but first she broke part off and handed it to the child. "Mary, may I ask a question?"

"Aye."

"Why did the Buchannans hate Arabella?"

Mary hesitated to answer, but someone would tell Kristin eventually, so it might as well come from her. "Arabella was not our first mistress."

"Truly? I had not guessed that."

"The first was a lass of only fourteen, who loved Hendry very much and whom the clan loved in return. No finer lass ever there was in the world."

"What happened to her?"

"She hung herself."

Kristin gasped. "Why?"

"Arabella."

"Oh…no." Kristin bowed her head. "My mother hurt so many. How could she? Had she no heart at all?"

"Not that I saw." Mary quickly drew in a breath. "Forgive me, she was your mother and I should not…"

"Thank you for being honest with me." No wonder, Kristin thought, as she ate her bread. Arabella began her life here under a sky she could not brighten no matter what she did. On the other hand, her mother deserved to be unhappy. She must have loved Hendry very much to live in such misery, and Kristin wasn't sure she could love any man that much, not even Tavan.

"There is gossip," Mary timidly said, as she took a seat at the table.

Kristin rolled her eyes. "More than you know. What have you heard?"

"'Tis said your mother gave over another daughter."

"Another daughter? Have they any proof?"

"Arabella was with child often, perhaps every year or so, just as all lasses are. Yet only five survived…and you."

"But if she gave more than me away, how? I mean, how could she manage to give more children away without Hendry knowing?"

Mary slowly shook her head. "Kristin, when a lass gives birth, she is alone in a room…save for one other."

"A midwife helped her. Can you take me to your midwife?"

"Nay, Arabella would have none other than a MacGreagor midwife."

"A MacGrea…?" Her mouth dropped. "I could have a sister and perhaps even a brother living in my very own clan without my knowing." Kristin took a deep breath and absentmindedly kissed the top of the little boy's head.

"Aye, and without Hendry knowing it."

"True, I pray he never finds out. We shall surely have a war if he does."

"He'll not hear it from any of us."

Kristin reached out and took Mary's hand. "Tell me, how does a mother decide which child to keep and which to shed herself of?"

"I do not know. I could give no child away."

"Better still, how could Hendry let her?"

"Laird Buchannan has always refused to look upon the dead. If she claimed the child died, then he would not ask to see it and none would be the wiser," answered Mary.

"But others would wash and view the body, would they not? 'Tis how it is done in our village."

"Had Arabella been loved, perhaps, but…"

"She was not loved, she was loathed." After a long, thoughtful silence, Kristin muttered, "How shall I ever understand her?"

*

"What did you talk about?" Sharla demanded.

Jenae was barely home long enough to take her horse to pasture and walk back up the glen, before Sharla was hot on her heels. Too late Jenae realized she should have found a reason to stay with the horse; Sharla was less fond of horses than she was of the elders. "We talked of nothing important; cows and sheep, mostly."

"Cows? You spent the day with the most handsome lad in the clan and you talked of cows? Did he kiss you?"

Jenae stopped walking and turned to stare at her friend. "He has not come back yet?"

"I have not seen him."

"If you must know, we parted ways and he went to see Samuel."

"Oh. Well then, did you ask him to go with you or did he ask you?"

"Neither. We just happened to be going the same way. Sharla, must you know every detail? I assure you I have not yet won the wager. He favors Kristin, just as I said."

"Kristin is gone and she is not coming back."

"You do not know that."

"Perhaps not, but I believe it. Why would the daughter of a laird come back to work the land, when she could have an easy life with the Buchannans. I would not, I assure you."

"I doubt you would," said Jenae.

"Besides, we are better off without Kristin. A lass like that tempts the lads to commit adultery."

"And the lads have no say in the matter?"

"Nay, they cannot resist."

"Sharla, who fills your head with such thoughts as these? 'Tis a lie."

"My mother says it is so, and she would not lie. Arabella tempted many a lad and Kristin will be just like her."

"Well my mother says a lad can resist as well as a lass. If he commits adultery, the blame is his as well as hers."

"Not with one such as Arabella in our midst. I shall be happy never to see Kristin again. If she is gone when we take husbands, we shall not have that worry." Sharla felt a rain drop on her head and looked up. "We best get inside."

"Aye, we best," Jenae agreed, hurrying off in a different direction.

CHAPTER VIII

Samuel stood outside Sile's door and hesitated to knock, but what could he do? He half hoped she was not there, and he could simply leave the bag of vegetables outside her cottage and avoid seeing her altogether. Unfortunately, when he lightly knocked, she quickly answered, as if she already knew he was there. Perhaps she did. Everyone said she liked to sit near her window and watch the people walk by. It was unnatural, to his way of thinking. She looked happy to see him and he was immediately offended. "It means nothing, Tavan said to bring it." He handed her the sack, quickly turned and walked on down the path.

"S-s-stupid...l-l-lad," Sile muttered as she watched him go. "T-t-thinks...I f-f-fancy him...he d-d-does." Just as the rain began to come down, she stepped back inside her cottage and closed the door.

The spies sent to check on Kristin stayed the night in the forest and then came home They reported Kristin was well, they saw her for themselves and it eased Tavan's mind.

"She wears Buchannan colors," one of the guards muttered.

Sawney nodded. "'Tis wise to honor her father that way." He dismissed the guards and stayed where he had been most of the day -

alone with Tavan trying to decide what to do.

"So long as she does not intend to wear Buchannan colors always," Tavan muttered.

"'Tis her choice," Sawney reminded him. "If she stays 'tis because she does not love you."

"Loving me is her choice, but what is Samuel to do? Must he go to the Buchannan village when he desires to see her? He hides his misery well, Father, but he suffers. I can see it in his eyes." Tavan had been toying with an idea and now seemed the time to suggest it. "I will go to see her in a day or two. If I go, Laird Buchannan will not see it as a threat. He is aware Kristin and I are friends and perhaps he even expects it."

"Nay, I will not allow it. I'll not send my son without a full guard and *that*, Laird Buchanan would consider a threat. Besides, if you go, he will guess we do not trust him to bring her back."

Tavan sighed. "You are right, Father, but there must be something we can do. She must be told how her father suffers."

"I am certain she knows, son. You would know if I suffered the loss of you. I recall when your Aunt Paisley married into another clan. I was quite young and missed her terribly."

"Aye, but you could go see her often."

"True." Sawney wistfully looked up at the ceiling. "I often wonder how a lad can give a daughter away, even to make an alliance with another clan. I could not do it."

Tavan chuckled, "Not even Colina?"

"Especially Colina. Who would entertain us of an evening if not your sister?" Not since Kristin went away had Tavan picked up his carving, and just now, Sawney wished he would. "You were seen with Jenae this morning."

Tavan rolled his eyes, "Do you set spies to watch me?"

"Aye."

Tavan laughed. "I suspected as much. Perhaps I should ride with a different lass each day, so you will have something new to ponder."

"Shall I help you arrange that?"

Tavan stood up, patted his father on the shoulder and started for the door. "I can manage."

Tavan wasn't outside long before he spotted Jenae in the glen. She seemed to be intently watching something and he was intrigued. He quietly walked to her and was by her side when he realized what it was. A crouching cat near the edge of the forest had its eyes glued on a mouse. Not far from a tree, the mouse sat on its hind legs nibbling on a morsel of stolen bread, and seemed oblivious to the danger.

When she noticed Tavan, Jenae smiled. Still, she wanted to see if the mouse would spot the cat in time. The cat looked frozen in a position poised to strike, but she doubted it was close enough. Could the cat outrun the mouse if it crept closer and gave its position away? She could not guess. There was much to learn from the behavior of animals and the quandary fascinated Jenae.

"Oh there you are," Sharla abruptly said behind them. The startled cat scurried away and when the mouse saw the cat finally, it raced into the forest.

"What?" Sharla asked when both Jenae and Tavan turned to stare at her.

"'Twas nothing important," Jenae managed to say.

Sharla was undaunted by their frowns. "Have you heard? Samuel took food to Sile last night."

"Why do you find that of note?" Tavan asked.

"Well, everyone thought he would be too mournful…over the death of his dreadful wife, I mean. But nay, he has already set his sights on Sile."

"Set his sights?" Jenae asked.

"Tis true, he took her the first of the harvest, which everyone knows is the best. First fruits are always the best, even God says so."

Tavan was horrified. The last thing he wanted was to bring any sort of shame or suspicion down on Samuel. "He took food to Sile because I asked him to."

"Oh," said Sharla. "Why would you do that?"

He could not hide his irritation. "Did you know Sile is not strong enough to open the storehouse door?"

"Aye, everyone knows."

"And you do not help her?"

Taken aback by his harsh demeanor, Sharla was certain he was accusing her. "I help her."

"See that you do. No MacGreagor lass should have to go to the storehouse in the night, for lack of food in the day." Before he completely lost his temper, Tavan left.

Sharla slowly turned her disfavor on Jenae, "You told him?"

"I did not, but I am not the only one who has seen you refuse to help her."

"Then Sile told him, and that is why he is angered."

"Or perhaps he did not find what you said pleasing."

"What? I said nothing wrong…oh, you mean about Samuel. Even if I misspoke, I am not the first to say it. Samuel could have sent someone else with the food, you know. I'd not be surprised if he truly fancies her, even though…s-s-she…talks…t-t-too…slow."

"Sharla, you are cruel. Sile cannot help the way she talks any more than you can help having yellow hair."

"What is wrong with yellow hair?"

Jenae stared at her dense friend and could not help a little jab. "Everyone knows dark hair is far more fetching."

"They do not. My mother said a lad will like a lass with light hair far sooner than one with dark."

Jenae decided not to mention that Sharla's mother had dark hair.

*

By the fourth day, Kristin was bored. The cleaning was done; she had walked all the paths, and met as many people as would talk to her. Her father's friends and his drunkenness each night kept her awake, and she was beginning to sleep as late as he did. For two days she carefully watched Hendry, trying to determine exactly what kind of man he was, yet he gave her little hint as to his real personality. Hendry seemed a bit too cunning to be as stupid as she first suspected, yet there was so much he closed his eyes to. Why? What makes a man allow himself to look foolish in the eyes of his followers?

What she wanted most was to talk it all over with Tavan. He was there from the beginning and he would help her sort out all her confusion. She longed to go home, but she longed to stay too…at least until she knew all there was to know about her blood parents.

The sun was high in the sky when Kristin crawled out of bed and got dressed. Her mind seemed a little foggy and for a moment, she was tempted just to lie back down. Less wine and more water, she decided, and a long walk in the forest would do no harm. Already she could hear men talking in the great hall, but it was not until she reached the bottom flight of stairs, that she heard her name.

"You are claiming my daughter?" Hendry asked.

"I am."

Cautiously, Kristin peeked around the corner so she could see who it was, but the man had his back to her. Michael and three other men, none of whom she recognized, stood watching.

"You shall not have her," Hendry said. He calmly set his morning gobbet of wine on the table.

"I am not worthy?" the man asked, his voice beginning to rise.

"You are as worthy as any lad, but Kristin is saved for another."

"What other?"

Kristin was happy to hear that her father was saving her for Tavan, although she left that quite unsettled. Nevertheless, Tavan was her choice and she hoped she would be Tavan's choice as well. Now that she had little to do, she spent a lot of time missing Tavan. Soon, she prayed, she would be back in his arms.

"Never you mind what other," said Hendry.

"I've as much right to claim..."

Hendry gritted his teeth. "I said, *nay!*"

"I call you out, Hendry Buchannan."

Hendry stared at the determined man standing before him. "You wish to die...over a lass?"

"Let me kill him, Father," Kristin said, boldly starting down the stairs. At last, the man turned and this one she did recognize. It was Padrig, the same man who dared to put his hand on her knee two nights before.

Padrig found her threat laughable. "*You...kill me?*"

"Doubt it if you will, but I warn you, I fight as well as any lad." Halfway down the stairs, she pulled her dagger, took the tip in her left hand and abruptly threw it.

Padrig heard the sound as it whizzed past his right ear and then turned to see where it landed. To his amazement, the dagger was lodged in the top apple in a bowl. He quickly turned back, just in case she had drawn her sword as well, and watched her calmly come down the stairs. He kept his eyes on her as she walked across the great hall and retrieved her dagger.

Kristin tightly gripped it as though she meant to stab him, walked to Padrig and with his eyes held in hers, wiped the apple juice off on his sleeve. "You'd not like being married to me. You might have your way with me once, but a lad must sleep and then...I would have my way with you." She put her dagger back in her sheath and headed for the door.

"Where are you going?" Hendry asked.

"Out."

*

For years, the triplets went fishing together each Thursday. They enjoyed the practice far more often than once in a week in the past, but that was before Patrick and Callum took wives and began families. With the river still lower than normal, they rode leisurely upriver to a place where the beavers had part of the water dammed.

"I say 'tis Sharla," Patrick said, dismounting, and then letting his horse drink from the cool river.

Tavan did the same and looked around for a good rock to sit on. "'Tis Sharla what?"

"'Tis Sharla you fancy."

Callum could not resist poking a little fun at his brother too. "I say, 'tis Jenae."

Tavan rolled his eyes. "Tell Father I fancy both and Kristin. That should give him something to ponder for a while."

As soon as his horse finished drinking, Callum tied him to a tree. "You would do well to marry Jenae, she is very pleasing."

"You would do well not to tell me who to marry. I did not interfere when you took a wife," said Tavan.

Patrick shared a grin with Callum before he said, "Only because you were captured at the time."

Tavan's greatest embarrassment was getting captured by the king's men and being accused of treason. Had it not been for the king's attachment to his brothers, he would have been executed and they were not about to let him forget it. "Am I never to live that down?"

"Never," both of Tavan's brothers said at the same time.

Tavan's mind wasn't much into fishing, so he sat down on a rock instead and just watched the river water flow to a sea he had never seen. The air smelled fresh, the second rain served to almost completely revive the lushness of the land, and the birds chirped happily in the trees. Soon, he noticed his brothers were not preparing their lines. "You do not wish to fish?"

"Nay, we have something to tell you," said Patrick.

"More bad news? I do not care to hear it."

Callum picked up a small rock and skipped it across the river. "You will want to hear this. Murdina had more than one child."

"Murdina, Arabella's mother?" Tavan asked.

"Aye and you cannot guess who he is," said Patrick.

"Who?" asked Tavan.

"Gordon," Patrick answered.

Tavan was shocked. "Gordon is Arabella's brother? Who said it?"

Callum skipped another rock across the water before he answered. "I got it from Fib, who got it from Nonie, who got it from Jernoot, the elder midwife."

"Then Kristin has an uncle?" Tavan asked. "Why did we not know that?"

"If you were Murdina's son, and you knew not who your father was, would you claim it?"

Tavan thought about that for a moment. "Perhaps not. Does everyone know?"

"They will soon enough," said Patrick. "'Tis no wonder Gordon is so..."

"Annoyed constantly?" Callum asked.

"True, he is annoyed more often than most," said Patrick. "Did you see the look in his eyes when he told us about Arabella leaving Kristin with Samuel? He seemed to greatly resent it and her for doing it."

Tavan watched the wind push a fluffy white cloud across the sky. "Perhaps he was pleased when Arabella left Samuel, but then she brought Kristin here and the child was a constant reminder."

"That must be it," said Patrick. "I cannot think what it must be like not knowing who fathered me. To hear Gordon tell it, Murdina...his mother, cared not who she bedded."

"I wonder..." Callum started to say.

"What?" Tavan asked.

"Could a lad kill his mother for denying him a rightful father?" Patrick answered.

That thought kept all three triplets deep in thought for several moments. "Gordon always suspected Arabella did it, but now I am inclined to think Gordon killed her," Callum said.

"Aye, but Murdina might have run off, or was captured by lads in another clan. We cannot know for certain she is dead."

"True, but just yesterday Gordon claimed his sister killed her. Why claim she was killed unless he knew she was dead?"

"By his own words..." Patrick muttered. "Should we tell father?"

Tavan finally smiled. "Do you truly suppose he does not already know? If he knew Kristin was Arabella's daughter, he surely knows Gordon is Arabella's brother."

"I wonder what else he knows," Callum said.

Tavan reached for his brother's hand and let Callum pull him up. "I believe we are still too young to hear it all."

"Speaking of Father," said Patrick, "if we go home with no fish, his questions will be endless."

*

If a man was to feel true terror, the worst would come from a wife who threatened to kill him in the night. Kristin was right to threaten in that way, and Michael was certain she would have no more trouble with Padrig…or any other lad, for that matter. As he had before, Michael followed Kristin into the forest, watched her choose flowers and made certain she was safe.

"Michael, how many brothers and sister do you suppose I truly had?"

"I did not count." He knew the question was coming and if Mary thought to be truthful with Kristin, he might as well too…at least on unimportant matters.

"I am seventeen and I was the first. If she had one a year and five died, that leaves how many?"

Michael had a sharp mind for numbers and quickly answered. "Twelve."

Her eyes widened. "Twelve?"

"There might have been a year or two when she did not give birth. I am not certain as I am your elder by only three years."

"I see, then eight or nine perhaps."

"Two or three might truly have passed."

"That is so. Then I shall count myself fortunate to have one or two yet living."

She moved to the next bush and examined it. "There is but one way to learn what happened to them. I will ask the midwife when I go home."

"You wish to go home?"

"Do not mistake my meaning, I do not hate it here, but I miss my father…Samuel very much. I miss the dogs and the cows and even the meanest bull on God's earth." Kristin was pleased when he smiled finally. He always seemed so serious, but she supposed he took his position seriously. "There is a lad I favor."

"Is there?"

"Aye, his name is Tavan."

"Tavan, I have heard that name"

"He was with me when Hendry came. Tavan is one of the triplets."

"Ah, I met his brothers then. They seem fine lads."

"They are very fine lads. Michael, Hendry does not intend to take me back, does he?"

He was caught completely off guard. "What?"

"Do not fret; I shall not insist you answer. I shall know the truth soon enough."

*

Indeed, the first fruits of the garden were ready to pick and all the MacGreagors were excited to help. Nevertheless, Sawney posted extra guards just in case the Buchannans thought to strike first. It was normally a happy time, even with such back breaking work as bending down and digging carrots out of the ground. Occasionally, the flute player would pause to play a tune, which was the signal to rest, and many sat down precisely where they were. When the music stopped, they returned to the work.

What they enjoyed most was watching to see which unmarried man would offer to carry heavy baskets for the unmarried women. The flirting and particular looks shared, gave rise to numerous amounts of gossip and speculation, which could possibly last well into winter.

Baskets made of heather were filled to the brim and loaded on carts to be hauled to the storehouses, except of course, that which went to tithe the church. In a plentiful year, the tithe was happily given, but this year the amount of the tithe depended on how much damage the drought had caused. The gardeners constantly monitored the amount, and when they gave Sawney the nod, men were assigned to take the carts off to the nearest Abby. No one ever accosted men in these circumstances, for stealing from the church was forbidden in all the clans. Nevertheless, this was not a usual year and Sawney doubled the guards just in case.

Sometimes Tavan worked beside Jenae and other times not. She was not quite certain if it was intentional, but not once did she see him near Sharla. It thrilled her and often made the work seem less strenuous. She was winning the wager; she was sure of it. Jenae wondered what she would do if Tavan actually chose her and was glad the courting ritual would be put off until after all the harvest was in. She liked Tavan, but love was something else again. Exhausted, she stood up, put her hands in the small of her painful back and arched it.

"This will help," Tavan said behind her. He untied his flask and offered his wine to her.

Jenae smiled. "I fear it would take three or four flasks to ease this pain."

"I do not wonder. You have hardly stopped all day."

She took the flask, tipped it up and drank her fill. "The days are getting shorter and the leaves are beginning to turn."

Tavan had not noticed and turned to survey the forest. She was right and soon, the leaves would be showing their glorious reds and yellows. "They rest in winter, Father says."

"Aye, that is what my mother says as well."

"How does she do?" he asked.

"I fear we shall lose her soon. Will you think ill of me if I say, I shall not be sorry to see her suffering end?"

He took the flask back, drank a few swallows and tied it to his belt. When he looked up, Jenae was back on her knees with tears in her eyes, picking pea pods and putting them in the basket beside her. He quickly knelt down and took her in his arms.

Sawney saw what he thought was affection and smiled. Sharla thought the same and narrowed her eyes. She marched straight down the row and stood next to Jenae with her hands on her hips. "What's this?"

While Jenae tried to wipe her tears away, Tavan looked up at Sharla and did not hide his displeasure. "She fears her mother will die."

"Oh, well, everyone's mother must die sometime."

Tavan could not think of anything the least bit pleasant to say, stood up, helped Jenae stand, and then took her hand. "Come, you need to rest and I need to calm my anger."

"What is the matter with him?" Sharla asked. Jenae, she noticed, did not bother to answer.

*

The next day, Jenae did not join in the harvest. Her mother died in the night and everyone mourned the loss. Tavan found it disheartening not to have her in the gardens, and had not before realized how often he kept an eye on her. Now, a place filled with people seemed empty and lonesome. Sharla was there, but he kept a good distance from her the entire day.

*

The Buchannans were tending their harvest as well, but theirs was an altogether different arrangement. The men did all the picking, and carried the baskets inside the fence, while the women sorted, filled the sacks and put them in the storehouses.

Just as all the clans did, vegetables and fruits that could be dried, were cut into small pieces and spread out on tables. The older children used large fans to keep the flies away, and dreamed of cold winter days when the food would be soaked in water, and revitalized for hot evening meals. For the next month or two, the dried food would be off limits and more often than not, their pots would be filled with carrots and turnips, whether the children liked it or not.

Kristin helped, but she found harvest without flirting and a flute player dull. On the other hand, when the Buchannan women were alone, they took every opportunity to talk about men, although sometimes they began a sentence, realized she was near, and did not finish it. Kristin was getting used to that.

Their crops fared better than the MacGreagors, and the share they sent off to the Abby was quite large. Hendry managed to make himself scarce, which did not impress Kristin in the least. More and more, she found herself comparing Hendry to Sawney, and the Buchannans to the MacGreagors. Twice she had occasion to be in the company of Padrig, but he said nothing and neither did she.

*

Tavan knew the people would talk, especially his father, but as soon as he finished bathing, he went to pay his respects to Jenae and her father. He viewed the peaceful face of the woman already in her box on the table, closed his eyes and bowed his head for a time. There was little he could say of comfort, but when Jenae came to him, he gladly opened his arms just as dozens of other men had during the day. It was the first time Tavan realized she was an only child.

"She does not suffer now," she whispered, as though she simply continued the conversation they began the day before.

"I am glad. What can I do to ease your grief?"

"Nothing, there is nothing to be done." She pulled away and went back to stand beside her father. "How goes the harvest?"

"We are to wait a day or two for more to ripen."

"I see." She could not think of anything else to say, watched as Tavan nodded to her father, and then left.

*

On the third day, nearly the entire clan walked behind Jenae and her father, while stout men carried her mother's box from their cottage to the graveyard. Jenae gave her full attention to her father and ignored everyone else, especially Sharla. She doubted they would ever be friends again.

The next morning, she and her father went to help bring in the rest of the harvest. Work was always the best way to pass the time and distract themselves from the grief. All day, she kept a close watch on her father, while Tavan kept a close watch on her. If Jenae noticed how attentive Tavan was, she did not let on. Her mind and her heart were still too heavy.

Sawney, on the other hand, became more and more convinced Kristin would not be the one Tavan chose for a wife. Still, he could not tell if Jenae felt any affection at all for his son. She did not look for him and only looked directly at Tavan when necessary. Twice, Mackinzie had to nudge Sawney, and remind her husband he was to help with the harvest instead of watching Tavan. Begrudgingly, Laird MacGreagor went back to loading carts, but keeping his mind on the work never lasted long.

*

Sharla was not at all pleased with the attention Jenae was getting from Tavan. Jenae would not look at her…her best friend for all these years and it irked Sharla no end. It was no big loss, she decided. There were other friends, and even though she did not like some of them, they might be useful. More importantly, if she was to get any notice at all from Tavan, she had to find a way to separate him from Jenae.

It was harder work, but Sharla left the rows of peas in favor of the cabbage patch, and began to pull the dirty, sunburned outer leaves off a head of cabbage before putting it in a basket. Beside her, Senga was doing the same. "I came to say, I was wrong about Parlan, He favors you and not me."

Senga's eyes brightened. "Truly?"

"Truly. I was mistaken and I hope you will forgive me."

Senga tossed a head of cabbage into the basket and threw her arms around Sharla. "Of course I forgive you. You have made me very happy."

Sharla was not that fond of being hugged and quickly ended their embrace. "He will ask you to walk with him soon, I wager."

"I hope so."

"I am sure of it. Now, who do you suppose Colina will choose? I say it will be Alec."

"Alec? Do you think so?"

"I do." Sharla went back to her work and pretended not to have a care in the world. "The lads set a beef and a hog in the ground to cook this morning. The harvest is near at end, finally, and are we not glad of that?"

"Aye, never have I hurt as bad as this. I ache into the night, even."

"So do I." Again, she pretended to happily continue the work. Then she leaned closer to Senga. "Have you heard?"

"What?"

Sharla cupped her hands and whispered in Senga's ear.

*

It was late, the evening meal was finished and Jenae had already washed their bowls and put them away when there was a knock at the door of their small cottage. As soon as her father opened the door, she was surprised to find Tavan waiting to be invited in.

"What brings you out this late at night?" Jenae's father asked.

"I've a bit of bad news. Might I come in?"

"Of course," said Jenae. She took a seat at the table and waited for Tavan and her father to do the same. "What is it?"

"Tis not an easy thing to tell. 'Tis said you and I…were seen going into the forest together after dark."

Jenae caught her breath. Horrified, she watched as her father slumped in his chair. "Do not believe it, 'tis a lie, Father."

"Indeed," said Tavan, "and I think we know who began it."

"Sharla," Jenae whispered. "She has outdone herself this time. Do others believe it?"

"I have denied it, but who can say if they believe me or her?" answered Tavan. "Sharla named no night. Therefore we cannot prove where we were at the time."

Jenae stared at the table for a moment, gathered her courage and then looked at Tavan. "It was a wager, you see. Sharla hoped you would choose her, and I...well, I said you would likely choose me as her. I do not recall what else was said, but we placed a wager on it."

"Oh, I see," said Tavan.

"Do forgive me, I was only...I found her particularly disagreeable that day, is all. I should not have done it and I meant no harm."

"No harm done...until now and I fear the harm is to you."

"I shall have a word with Sharla's mother," Janae's father muttered.

Tavan tried to comfort the man with a sly smile. "Nay, I've a better idea."

*

A week had passed since Kristin arrived, everyone was tired after the harvest, and still the men gathered in Hendry's great hall to drink and enjoy their nightly merriment. Kristin was exasperated with the whole lot of them. Did they not ever sleep? It was this part of her father's life she learned to hate quickly. Michael stayed not far from her, in case she thought to kill a man for touching her, she guessed, and for that she was grateful. It would take little to set her off.

Some evenings she believed Hendry was pretending to be drunk, but more often than not, he truly was. How easy it must have been for Arabella to slip out early in the morning, go see her other family, and then come back before Hendry was aware. Very easy indeed, since she slept in a different bed. The clan was probably glad to have her gone and did not bother to report her absence. Kristin was right in the very beginning -- Hendry truly was a stupid man, and how he survived this long as laird was beyond her. Perhaps few others truly wanted the position.

*

Laird Buchannan slept in a bed as large as Arabella's and abruptly awoke to find Michael sitting in a chair on the other side of his bedchamber watching him. "What…what is it?"

"You said to report as soon as the lads came back."

"So I did." Hendry struggled to rid himself of the covers and sit up on the edge of the bed. Still fully dressed he twisted his body, pulled his dagger out of its sheath and tossed it on the floor. "Can the lads not remove it when I am put to bed. 'Tis painful." Only then did he turn his attention back to Michael. "Go on, what have they to report?"

"The MacGreagor night guards sleep instead of watch."

Hendry was suddenly fully awake. "They sleep?"

"I doubt they mean to, but 'tis hard to please a wife and children, and then keep watch all night."

"I suppose it is at that. Thankfully we have a fence and towers to keep us safe. Is there more?"

Michael stood up. "Not yet, but we've another week still."

*

Sharla and Senga were happily walking and talking when Sharla spotted Jenae and Tavan farther down the glen. How she would have loved being able to hear what they were discussing, but they were too far away. Tavan stood with his legs apart, his arms folded and a look of torment on his face. Jenae seemed upset about something and Sharla pulled Senga to a stop so she could watch.

Considering the look on their faces, Sharla guessed Tavan was telling her about the latest gossip. It was clear Jenae was beginning to cry, but when Tavan reached for her, Jenae shook him off and shouted, "Dare you touch me?"

Jenae turned and ran back up the glen. She ignored the look of satisfaction on Sharla's face, turned up a path and went to her cottage. Once inside, she wiped her tears away and went into her father's arms.

"'Tis done?" he asked.

"Aye, 'tis done."

*

Sharla had no idea just how long it would take Tavan to get beyond any feelings he had for Jenae. It would be another day or two before the last of the MacGreagor harvest was dried and packed in the storehouse. By then, the meat in the pits would be fully cooked and the harvest celebration could begin. That should be more than enough time, Sharla decided, and therefore, she would not stand in the courtyard with the other unmarried women until after the festival. Her plan had to be very subtle indeed. Yet, that afternoon, he seemed to be looking at her occasionally and she wondered if he could have recovered so soon. Men were such odd creatures.

When evening finally arrived, Sharla strolled along the outside of the short wall, and was pleased when Parlan finally had the courage to ask Senga to walk with him. Alec asked Colina to walk, but she turned him down. What was wrong with Tavan's sister, anyway?

Deep in thought, she stopped and folded her arms. In the past, she had Jenae's company during the evening courting. Now that everyone had heard the gossip, Jenae dared not show her face, save for when it was necessary. No matter, once Sharla was Tavan's wife, Tavan's family would become her company.

"Are you lost?" Tavan asked.

Startled to find him so near, it took a moment to regain her composure. "Lost? How can I be lost in a courtyard I have known all my life?"

"You look a bit lost."

She smiled, "Well if I do, it is because not one stone has been set in the castle you vowed to build for me."

"You are right; I have neglected the matter completely."

"I suppose the harvest got in the way. 'Tis as good excuse as any."

"I am pleased you agree." It was almost painful to smile at her, but he reminded himself it was for Jenae. Still it would take getting used to, considering the anger he still felt, so he simply nodded and went to join his brothers.

*

Two floors above the MacGreagor great hall, Sawney shook his head. "Now what is the lad up to? I could have sworn he preferred Jenae, but now he…"

"My love," Mackinzie said, coming to stand beside him at the window. "I am not convinced he has forgotten Kristin."

"Why not? He has not spoken of her in days."

"Aye, but he does not carve either. He has not even taken it to the

Carley cottage, where he may work in peace. If your son is in love, it is with Kristin."

Sawney put his arms around his wife. "He is *my* son now, is he?" She giggled until he lowered his lips to hers and passionately kissed her.

*

Wood carving was the last thing on Tavan's mind when he set the candle down in the middle of the small table in the Carley cottage. Jenae was hurt and he blamed himself for it. He should have considered what others would think when he gave his attention to her alone. They thought he preferred her, how could they think otherwise?

Tavan sat down on the bed and began to unlace his shoes. His muscles were still sore, as he suspected everyone else's were. There were liniments he could use, but some smelled, some were oily and some did no good that he could tell. He was glad not to be in the Keep where his mother could fuss over him.

He took off his other shoe, put it with the first and set them beside the bed, where he could easily find them. Then he took off his belt and kilt, laid them across the back of a chair, blew out the candle and climbed into bed. He folded his arms behind his head and closed his eyes.

He was bothered by what Jenae told him, but he understood how it happened - Sharla could be very irksome. Still, it was all a trick, a wager between Jenae and Sharla to gain his favor. There was no doubt which of the two he would have chosen, if only between those two; Sharla was his least favorite of all the MacGreagor women.

Still, he liked the new friendship he had, or thought he had, with

Jenae. If she had no real affection for him, why did it bother him so? Wasn't it Kristin he thought about constantly? His pride was bruised and that was all, he decided as he turned over and went to sleep.

*

Kristin could not figure out what was wrong. She awoke for a moment, but the temptation to go back to sleep was overwhelming and she easily succumbed to it. She dreamed of going home and of the dogs running to greet her the way they did Sile. Somewhere in her dream, Tavan was frowning and she could not understand why. Michael was there too, looking somber and Michael's wife, Mary, was crying. Tavan kept calling her name, but she did not have the strength to answer.

"Kristin…Kristin, wake up!"

At last, she lifted her head and looked at him. There seemed to be a dark cloud over her eyes with only a narrow opening to see through. She tried hard to focus on the face of the man standing at the end of the bed, but it took a while. "Michael?"

"Aye."

"What…?" It was then she noticed Mary sitting on the bed next to her, holding her hand.

"You have been poisoned, we think," Mary whispered.

"Poisoned?" She laid her head back down and closed her eyes to try to keep the room from spinning. 'Tis a dreadful way to die."

"We shall not let you die," Michael said, suddenly standing beside her bed."

"I wish to go home."

"I do not blame you," said Mary. "'Tis the same way your mother died, we see that now. Hendry's first wife's brother did it, we think."

"Let me die...I beg of you."

"Fight Kristin, you must fight to live so you can kill the lad who did this," said Michael."

Kristin let her heavy eyelids close and moaned. "You kill him."

Michael smiled. "Nay, you must do it, 'tis the Buchannan way." He was lying, but he was willing to say anything to keep her from giving into death.

Mary tried to smile. "There is but one way to make you well, you must drink soap."

Kristin was suddenly far more awake. "Soap?"

"Aye," said Mary. "'Twill make you throw up."

Kristin groaned. "No doubt." She slowly looked around. It was the first time she noticed she was not in her own bed, nor even in the Keep. Another man sat at the table and the candle light made him look distorted, so she looked away.

"Michael brought you here in the night," Mary said.

Kristin put her hands on the top of her aching head. "Soap?" This time she gave in to the urge to go back to sleep.

Hendry was beside himself with worry. There was no room to pace in Michael's small cottage, so he was forced to sit in a chair and watch Mary fuss over Kristin. "If the MacGreagors hear of this, they will surely attack."

Michael filled a bowl with water, set it on the table and reached for some cloths. "Then they shall not hear of it."

Hendry shook his head. "Michael, when someone tries to poison the daughter of a laird, the whole world hears of it."

"What then? We must take her back to the Keep when she is well enough, and once they see how bad she looks, they will surely talk." For a drunkard, Hendry appeared to have all his faculties about him and Michael was grateful. He could use a little clear thinking from his laird just now. "Perhaps we should be the ones to tell the MacGreagors. That way they will not think we try to keep it from them."

Hendry gave that considerable thought. "They will want to come see for themselves."

"Aye, but by then, she will have recovered her health. Arabella always got better."

Hendry wrinkled his brow and stared at Michael. "Are you certain Arabella was poisoned?"

"Can there be any doubt? Does Kristin not suffer the same complaints?" asked Michael.

"But Arabella was unwell for weeks. Is there one so evil as to make a lass slowly die of poison?" Hendry closed his eyes and answered his own question, "Padrig."

Michael nodded. "That is what I think."

"I should have done away with him years ago. Why did he wait all these years to poison Arabella?"

"Perhaps it was you he wished to make suffer. Did he not watch you grieve the loss of your sons? Perhaps he wishes your grief to continue just as his does for his sister."

"Perhaps so." Hendry closed his eyes and bowed his head. "Michael, you are right. We must be the one to tell the MacGreagors and you must go. They will expect my second in command to carry news such as this. Go at first light. Once you are well away, I will carry Kristin to her bed and none but Mary shall tend her."

CHAPTER IX

On her father's advice, Jenae decided hiding made her look guilty. Taking a walk in the glen took all her courage and as she feared, everyone stayed clear of her. No matter, she walked to the farthest log along the edge of the glen, and sat down to watch the colts play. One, an all-white with black markings, was especially lively, running back and forth from its mother to one of the other colts, as if to tempt a hearty chase. The other colt was apparently more interested in a meal. Any other morning, it would have made her smile…but not this morning.

Several children distracted her for a little while, until she spotted Tavan talking to his brothers and looked away. He kept his distance as she expected, but it was almost impossible not to look at him, just to see if he was looking at her. How distressing it seemed to have him near, yet so far away. She folded her arms and tightened them for warmth. Did she love him and if she did, did he love Kristin instead?

Jenae always believed he loved Kristin, which made her casual flirtation with him seem harmless at the time. Now she sorely regretted it. She neglected to protect her own heart along the way. Now, after her trickery, he could hardly respect her let alone love her. What a mess she had made of everything.

*

Tavan ignored his brothers and barely heard a word either of them said. His mind was on the fastest way to relieve Jenae's distress. The sorrow on her face was unbearable and he longed to go to her and take her in his arms.

Suddenly, Callum grabbed his arm. "You must not."

"Not what?" Tavan asked.

"Go to her or even look at Jenae. Sharla is watching your every move."

Tavan lowered his eyes. "You are right, Sharla must think I have no feeling left for Jenae. Yet I hate seeing her suffer. Is there nothing we can do?"

Callum moved to block Tavan's view of Jenae. "I already have, your sister goes to sit with her."

Tavan looked around for Colina, smiled and playfully slapped Callum on the back. "Why did I not think of that?"

"Admit it, you are witless where lasses are concerned," said Callum.

Patrick grinned, "Not as witless as you, Callum. As I recall, you married only to save a lass from life with a very disagreeable lad. You did not even know Kylie's name."

"You are wrong brother, I knew her name but she did not know mine. I shall never forget…" Callum started to recall.

*

"Care for a bit of company?" Colina asked.

Jenae smiled. "You are very kind. Will you sit with me?"

"Only if you allow me to ask questions."

"Ask me anything you like."

Colina sat on the log next to her, stretched out her legs and folded her hands in her lap. "It is true my brother shamed you?"

"Nay, Tavan would never do that."

"That is what I think too."

"You do?"

"Of course I do. My brother is many things, but he would not do that."

"Thank you, I am happy someone believes us."

"And I am happy to have a new friend. You have no idea how many pretend to like me, just because I am my Father's daughter. It is exhausting."

"I had not realized that."

"And the lads as well. A laird's daughter is a fine catch, I have heard them say. I truly do not want to be caught like a fish on a hook."

Jenae laughed. "I do not blame you." She saw Tavan watching her and quickly lowered her eyes. Just now, perception was important for Sharla's sake, but did he have to laugh just after he looked at her?

"I see you ride off some mornings, where do you go?" Colina asked.

"I go to visit an uncle in the gardens."

"May I go with you?"

"Now?"

"Have you something better to do?"

Jenae stood up, offered Colina a hand and helped her stand. "I do not."

*

Sharla never could tell the triplets apart unless they were up close. Even with slightly different appearances, they all looked the same to her, especially when they were together. One had his back to her and she feared it was Tavan watching Jenae, but when they all laughed, she took a forgotten breath. Just then, the smoke from the meat pits drifted her way and she was forced to leave her seat on the short wall in favor of standing near the Keep. Then, Jenae and Colina headed for their horses and so did two of the triplets. Sharla held her breath. Was Tavan one of them?

She watched Colina try to shoo her brothers away, to no avail. No doubt Sawney would not let his precious daughter go off without protection and Jenae, Sharla noticed, was not objecting. Tavan was one of them, she was sure of it. There was little more to see and once they rode away, she'd lost track of the third triplet. Oh well, perhaps she might have more luck later.

"Do you wish to go with them?" Tavan asked, peeking around the corner of the Keep.

Sharla smiled. "Nay, I have gone with Jenae before and 'tis boring."

"Then what shall you do this bright and sunny day?"

"The same as always, I suppose - whatever my mother requires of me."

"I see." He paused to make certain he asked the question in just the right way. "Will you be walking in the glen later?"

Her smile could not have been more radiant. "If you like." With a light heart and a swelled head, she turned and went home.

*

Never had Sharla wanted to do her chores more quickly. The rain made the river water more abundant, and instead of having to go to the loch, she carried her basket to the river. Other women had the same idea, and she had to wait for one to finish, but she did not mind waiting. It would not do to return to the glen too soon. Even so, she would rather make short work of the wash if she could. When she was mistress of the MacGreagors, providing the clan chose Tavan, she would not have to do the wash ever again. What a happy day that would be.

Once the wash was finished, she hurried off to bathe with the other women in the loch and then concentrated on drying her hair and braiding it just so. At last, she was ready and walked into the glen. She expected Tavan to be waiting for her, but he was nowhere in sight. In an effort not to appear as though she was waiting for him, she went to find Senga to walk with. Senga was busy and so were all her other friends, so she could do nothing but wander around the glen all alone.

She watched the younger warriors practice their skills and almost laughed. They were a bungling lot and certain to hurt themselves or each other soon. Anyone watching would think the MacGreagors ill trained indeed. It occurred to her the older ones should be there too, just as they always were, but it was none of her concern. Pretending not to have a care in the world, she strolled across the glen to watch the children play. That too, she found exceedingly boring. Next, she stopped to watch the horses, even though she had no real interest in them either.

She might have been happy to see anyone at all come toward her, but not Tavan's youngest sister, Bardie. She did not find children to be fitting company for someone her age, but Bardie would have to do until the other women appeared.

Bardie walked with her for just a little while, before she said, "Tavan fancies you, I think." She was pleased to see she had Sharla's full attention.

"Does he?"

"Aye, he spoke of you at our evening meal last and he never speaks of any lass."

"What did he say?"

Just then, Mackinzie stepped out of the door of the Keep, called her and Bardie dashed away. As soon as she walked into the Keep, Tavan handed her a carved eagle she had been longing to call her own. She briefly hugged him and dashed up the stairs to put it in her bedchamber.

A smiling Tavan put his arm around his mother, hugged her and turned around...only to find his father with one eyebrow raised.

"What are you up to, son?" Sawney asked.

"Up to? I know not what you mean." Tavan went to his carving for the first time in days.

"You conspire with my wife and my daughter this day. And where, might I ask, are my other sons and Colina? You are up to something and I wish to know what it is."

"Father, you are not going to give me that speech again, are you?"

"What speech might that be?"

"The one about how *you* are the laird and you must know *everything*."

"I might."

Mackinzie grinned, went to her husband and sat in his lap, as much to show affection as to hold him down when she told him. "My love, you must not get upset."

Sawney quickly narrowed his eyes. "What?"

She paused for just a moment. "It is said Tavan took Jenae into the forest after dark."

"What?" Sawney nearly shouted.

She could feel his muscles tighten and his rage begin. "My love, here is what your son is up to." She put her cheek next to his and whispered in his ear.

*

Tavan knew his brothers would take care of Jenae, but the longer she suffered the worse he felt. Still, he had to wait until there were more people in the glen. "Father," Tavan said after his mother went upstairs, "If someone refused to help Sile open the door to the storehouse, what should the punishment be?"

Sawney was just beginning to calm down and turned in his chair to look at his son. "Sile cannot open it? Of course she cannot, I should have realized that. Are you saying you know of someone who would slight her?"

"I saw it myself just yesterday. Fib came along and opened it for her."

"I find such a thing unforgivable. What do you think the punishment should be?"

"I think such a person should be made to stand guard and open the door for everyone...for at least a week."

"Especially Sile?"

"Especially Sile."

Sawney shook his head, turned back around to face the door and hide his anger. "Sile never said a word, but then, she does not complain."

"Why did you never marry her off after her husband died?"

"If she desired a husband, I would have, but she clearly did not. I fear few, but I learned long ago not to upset Sile."

Tavan chuckled. "I shall never forget when she caught us..."

*

The longer she waited, the more irritated Sharla became. She was beginning to think there was some grand plan afoot, since not one of her friends came to talk to her. Jenae, Colina and Tavan's brother came back and set their horses free. That was a very good thing, in Sharla's opinion. Nothing would please her more than for Jenae to see Tavan walking with her.

Yet she still stood alone in the glen and it was a sure thing Jenae would not come to talk to her. She doubted Colina would either, now that she and Jenae seemed to be good friends. How dreary they looked, even with smiles on their faces, so dreary in fact, Sharla turned to look once more at the door of the Keep. At least the glen was beginning to fill with people, making it much easier to act coy and surprised when Tavan came to walk with her.

At last, Tavan came out. Yet he did not come directly to her, forcing her to wait even longer. Instead, he went to talk to Fib. Like her mother always said, men were impossible to understand when it came to love. Frustrated, she decided to visit the graveyard and look at the stones. The newest grave was that of Jenae's mother, so Sharla quickly moved on.

When she least expected it, she turned to see Tavan walking

straight for her. She smiled, lowered her gaze just the way her mother taught her to, and pretended to smooth the pleats in her skirt.

"I do hope I did not keep you waiting." Tavan said.

"Not at all," she lied.

He motioned toward the lower part of the glen. "Shall we?" He waited for her to nod and then clasped his hands behind his back. The last thing he wanted to do was touch her. "I fear your castle may be delayed again."

"How so?"

"Father has need of me just now."

"Oh, I forgot you are second in command. Well, if he must have you, I suppose he must."

"How large do you desire this castle be, once I begin to build it, that is?"

"Oh very large indeed. I desire eight rooms, if not ten."

"And will you fill them with a husband and children?"

She was surprised he got around to mentioning that quite so soon, but she was thrilled to hear it. "Of course. I'd not like living alone in such a large place."

"I see. And what sort of husband do you desire?"

"Well, he must be kind, loving and most of all keep himself only unto me."

"I desire the same in a wife…save for one other requirement."

"Which is?"

"Honesty. I could never marry a lass who lies."

Sharla stopped walking and stared at him. "I do not lie."

"Of course you do not, I did not mean you." He hit a nerve which was exactly what he hoped to do. "On the other hand, everyone lies. It cannot be helped from time to time. Even so, my wife will be of such a good nature, she will confess her lie should she find it has hurt someone." Sharla did not respond, so he started them walking again and let her think about it.

At length, Sharla said, "Perhaps she did not mean to lie."

"I am certain of it. Nevertheless, if someone is hurt, the wrong must be righted."

"Or you would not wish to marry her?"

"I would not, indeed could not, until she confessed."

She looked away for a time, and then turned to him with tears in her eyes. "Tavan, I have lied, but I did not mean to."

He almost felt sorry for her, but that passed quickly. "Then you must confess it to everyone."

"Everyone?"

"Aye, telling me alone would never do. The lass I marry must be worthy of honor." To emphasize his point, he folded his arms and kept his expression stern.

"Oh very well." Sharla quickly wiped her tears away and did not stop talking the whole time she walked beside him back to the village. "I never meant to hurt her, I only…"

As soon as they walked past, Tavan motioned for Jenae to follow. Soon Colina, Patrick, Callum, Bardie, Mackinzie and Sawney were walking behind them too. Once they got to the courtyard, Tavan whistled to gather the clan.

Sharla could not have been more nervous. The clan quickly gathered as if they'd been waiting, and for a moment she suspected they had. Her mother came, Senga and Parlan were there, and when she looked back, even Jenae was with them.

Thankfully, Tavan stayed by her side to give her courage. She decided to concentrate on only one thing - she would be his wife soon, all she had to do was confess.

"Tell them," Tavan whispered.

She hesitated and once more looked around. Laird MacGreagor was there and he might punish her, but...

"Tell them," Tavan whispered again.

Sharla took a very deep breath and spit it out. "I lied. I did not see Tavan take Jenae into the forest after dark. There, I confessed it." She had a glow on her face as she turned to see Tavan's approval, but her proud smile quickly faded. His glare was so fierce, she began to back away and it all became perfectly clear. He did not love her and never intended to make her his bride.

Suddenly, a faint, piercing whistle sounded at the far end of the glen and everyone turned to look. Seconds later, the whistle was repeated by closer guards in the forest, until it was loud enough to alert even those still in their cottages. Men ran forward, drew their swords prepared to defend the clan, and every eye watched a lone Buchannan race his horse at full speed toward the village.

It was just one man, but he could be the first of many and no one was willing to take a chance. As they had been trained, the women quickly gathered their children and headed for their hiding place in the hills, while Sawney's guard encircled him. Mackinzie refused to budge, so Alec and three others stood guard in front of Mackinzie, Bardie, Jenae and Colina.

Waiting next to his father, Tavan whispered, "Kristin."

*

Michael had not yet completely halted his horse when he swung down and ran toward Sawney. The MacGreagors protecting their laird closed ranks even tighter and made him stop short, yet he was able to look Sawney in the eye when he shouted, "She has been poisoned." He took care to keep his hands away from his weapons and waited for his words to sink in.

"You came alone?" Sawney asked.

Nearly out of breath, Michael answered, "Fear not, there are no others."

With Tavan and Gordon right behind him, Sawney parted his men and walked to Michael. "Is she dead?"

"Nay, we will not let her die and Hendry pledges not to let anyone near her save my wife. She is very ill, but she will recover."

"I must go to her," said Tavan. He started for his horse just as Sawney grabbed his arm.

"Son, I fear it is a trap."

"'Tis not a trap," said Michael, "I swear it."

"I believe him," said Gordon as he stepped forward. "He is Michael, the lad I told you about."

"The one you fish with?" Sawney asked.

"Aye."

"Then I believe him as well. Gordon, fetch Samuel and be quick about it. Tavan find Sile. If anyone can give Kristin the best care, 'tis Sile.

"Father, Sile greatly pains," Tavan argued.

"Then bring her best medicine and ask her how to use it."

Tavan wanted to just mount his horse and ride out, but he did as his father commanded. He raced across the courtyard, around the Keep and down the path.

Behind him, Sawney was still issuing orders. "Callum and Patrick will go with him. Errol bring fresh horses for the Buchannan, and Parlan, see they have full flasks of MacGreagor wine and water. I'll not have them poisoned too." Instantly, the men did as he said and after he told his warriors to stow their weapons, there was nothing left to do.

Michael took two more gulps of air and bowed. "I thank you, Laird MacGreagor. I feared you would cut me down."

"You are not yet safe. I cannot promise her father will not want to fight, but he is a sensible lad when he calms. Tell me what happened."

*

There was nothing Jenae could do but wait and watch. If she was worried about the triplets riding into possible danger, she thought Colina must be beside herself. She put her arm around her friend's waist to comfort her and Colina returned the gesture.

The horses were readied and it seemed to take forever, but Samuel and Gordan finally rode hard into the glen from the gardens. When Tavan came back with a small sack of medicines tied to his belt, he took only a moment to kiss his mother's cheek before he mounted his horse.

"Bring Kristin home," Sawney said.

"Aye, Father," said all three triplets.

Then it happened. Tavan turned, looked for Jenae, found her and nodded. A moment later, the triplets, Michael and Samuel rode down the glen and disappeared. What Tavan's nod meant exactly, Jenae was uncertain and it puzzled her greatly. It probably only meant he was happy her good reputation was restored. She'd forgotten all about that, but apparently he hadn't. At least now, they could be friends again.

His sons were barely out of sight when Sawney turned around and bellowed, "Sharla!"

*

It was nearly dark by the time the MacGreagors and Michael walked their horses through the tall wooden gates of the Buchannan village.

Hendry stood outside waiting for them and addressed his comments to Samuel, "She is better and asking for you."

The MacGreagors dismounted, handed their reins to the waiting boys and followed Hendry into the Buchannan great hall. None of the triplets noticed the people gawking at their towering size or their very similar appearance. Nor did they look around the place as they followed Hendry up the stairs, down the hall and up another staircase.

Hendry led them down another hall, stopped, softly knocked on a bedchamber door, and then waited for a small, pleasant woman to open it. Then he stood aside and let the MacGreagors enter.

"Father," Kristin whispered.

Samuel quickly crossed the dimly lit room and sat down next to her on the bed. She looked so small and frail in a bed that was far too large, and he had to force a smile to comfort his daughter. He gently wrapped his arms around her and lifted her to him, yet she was so weak, she could barely hug him back and it terrified him. "You must rest and get well, daughter."

She slightly nodded, and did not resist when he lay her back down. "I drank soap water."

"Soap?"

The worry lines were deep in his forehead when Mary came closer to explain. "It was to make her throw up the poison."

"I see." Samuel' smile was far more genuine this time. "Did it work?"

"Aye," Kristin answered.

"Then I am glad. Tavan came; do you wish to see him?"

"I…" She reached a shaky hand up to touch her hair.

"He will not mind, he is only happy you are alive." Samuel stood up, moved away and nodded for Tavan to take his place. His fondest wish was that she would marry Tavan, and Samuel motioned everyone out so they could be alone.

"I have missed you." Tavan said. He took her hand in his, leaned over and kissed the top of her forehead. Then he carefully sat down beside her. Her skin was a ghostly gray and if she was better now, he hated to think how she looked before. "Will you live?"

"Michael says I must. I am to kill the lad who did this to me, but I think Hendry already killed him."

He was relieved she was able to carry on a conversation. "Good, then I am saved the trouble. Sile sent some medicine."

"Is it soap?"

He chuckled. "Nay, but it tastes just as bad. Are you hungry?"

"A little."

"Good. Patrick and Callum came with me. I shall make them taste the food first, to be certain it is safe." He made her smile and that pleased him very much.

*

By the time Mary came back with a warm bowl of broth, and Tavan went back downstairs, Hendry was beginning to explain what happened. "Myra went to take Kristin some fresh water before she went to bed, and always before Kristin awoke when she entered, no matter how quiet Myra tried to be. Last night Kristin groaned instead. Myra suspected a spider bite, but could find no bites on Kristin, so she ran to get Michael."

"Then 'twas Michael who saved her?" asked Samuel.

"Aye, there be no better second than Michael in all of Scotland." Hendry watched each of the MacGreagors nod their appreciation to Michael.

A little embarrassed, Michael said, "We like Kristin well enough, but 'twould do the same for any lass."

"Kristin thinks you already executed the lad who did this. Is it true?" Tavan asked.

Hendry took a drink of his wine and nodded. "Aye, Padrig confessed. We did away with him this morning." Hendry looked as beaten down as any man could, when he bowed his head and closed his eyes.

Michael watched his laird carefully. Hendry, it appeared, was beginning to deal with the idea that three of his five sons need not have died, and it showed in his pained expression. Whatever else Laird Buchannan was, he truly loved Arabella's sons as much as he loved her. Would the man before him completely crumble after the

MacGreagors left, Michael wondered. Perhaps not, not as long as Kristin was here.

"Father said to bring her home," Tavan said, breaking the awkward silence.

Samuel shook his head. "I doubt she can survive the journey. We must wait."

"I agree," said Hendry. "She is safe here now, I will not let more harm come to her."

"Are there no others who hate you?" asked Samuel.

Hendry ignored Samuel's snide tone of voice. "Aye, plenty, and most are MacGraw."

"Tell us about the battle," Patrick said.

As men do, the MacGreagors eagerly asked questions and enjoyed hearing the answers. Michael listened, laughed when it was appropriate and noticed how cleverly his laird avoided the truth. Hendry did not mention that they nearly lost that battle, or that his last remaining sons were killed in the process. Padrig was commander of the warriors, and just now Michael wondered if Padrig truly did all he could to win that battle.

"You fear the MacGraw will attack?" Tavan asked.

"'Laird MacGraw is not fond of losing," Hendry answered. "Aye, he will attack."

"What will become of Kristin if…?" Samuel started.

"As soon as I know, I shall send her to you. Hopefully, she will be well enough by then. If not, we shall hide her in the forest. Fear not, Samuel, I do not wish harm on her any more than you do."

"Do they prepare to fight again?" asked Callum.

"Not that I am aware of."

Tavan frowned. "Have you no spies watching them?"

Hendry slyly smiled. "Should a laird confess his defenses to strangers?"

The elder man was shrewder than Tavan thought. "A second in command might hope the laird is witless enough to answer."

"A point well taken. Let me say only this: I shall know of it well before they attack. We knew you were coming before you were halfway here."

"But the MacGraw *will* attack?" asked Samuel.

Hendry paused for a minute. He aimed to use Kristin's poisoning to his advantage, by drawing her recovery out longer than necessary. Yet if the MacGreagors feared a MacGraw attack, they might try to take her with them now. "I assure you, Kristin will be safe. She is my daughter and I shall protect her."

"Like you did from the poison?" Samuel asked.

Hendry slumped his shoulders. "Calm yourself, Samuel. I had no forewarning of Padrig's treachery, but I will have ample time to see to her safety if the MacGraw are coming. They are not a quiet lot when they are on the move."

Samuel seemed a little more content with that answer. He would like watching the MacGraw fight the Buchannan, but not until he had Kristin home safely. He listened to Laird Buchannan continue to brag about his battle, and when he could not stomach being in the same room with Hendry any longer, he went back upstairs to be with Kristin.

Mary answered his soft knock on the door and smiled. "She is awake and managed to keep the broth down so far."

"I am relieved." He went inside and waited, but Mary did not close the door.

"Will you sit with her? I must see to my son for a little while."

"Of course, how do I thank you?"

"You need not, we like Kristin."

Samuel watched Mary go and then sat down on the bed beside Kristin again. Her eyes seemed a little brighter. "Is it very awful?"

"'Tis far from pleasant, but the cloud in my mind has gone away, finally."

He took her hand in his. "Do you forgive me for lying all these years? I could think of no way to tell you, not while Arabella was alive. You might have hated her and…"

"And she might have stayed away if I did?"

"Aye."

"Father, I know what missing someone is about now. How could I blame you for wanting to protect your heart from more hurt? If you could forgive her, who am I to deny you the same?"

"I am relieved." Samuel kissed her hand and then took a moment to look around the room. He spotted the goblet Hendry gave her, but didn't mention it. "So this is where your mother lived."

"Aye." Kristin saw no reason to tell him how miserable his wife had been; some things were best left unsaid. At least the place was clean now. "Mary and Michael have been very kind to me."

"And Hendry?"

"He is a bit of an odd duck."

"How so?"

Kristin smiled. "He called me Arabella."

"Ah, that *is* odd."

"'Twas only the once and I cured him of it."

Samuel laughed. "I wager you did."

"Tell me about home? Is the harvest in?"

"Aye, 'tis finished and we believe we have enough for winter. The wolves have gone back into the hills and…"

*

For the rest of the day and long into the night, Jenae tried to understand if Tavan's nod to her in particular meant he was happy her reputation was saved, he had forgiven her, or if it meant more than that. Certainly, she was in error in her effort to win the wager with Sharla, but her time with him came to mean so much more, at least to her. He seemed to enjoy the same things she liked, he cared that she mourned her mother, and helped her when it came to hauling the heavy baskets during harvest. Altogether, did it mean he fancied her, or was he just being kind? Now, he had run off to be with Kristin and that said much. It was Kristin he loved, not her and Jenae decided she best get used to it.

*

Tavan filled his goblet with more wine from his flask and pretended to be engrossed in Hendry's stories of the battle, but his thoughts soon drifted to Jenae. He would have liked watching the clan gather around her, now that Sharla had confessed. Furthermore, he should apologize for letting everyone think he preferred her. Then again, did he not feel those feelings for Jenae at the time? The truth be told, he missed her.

He tried to more closely examine the difference between his feelings for Kristin and those for Jenae. They were both very fine women in his opinion, both with just the right mixture of strength and kindness. Both were pleasing to look at, interesting to talk to and seemed happy to be with him. Was that love? He would wait and see, he decided. Just now he missed Jenae, but once he was home, would he miss Kristin again?

It was quiet in the MacGreagor village when Sawney climbed the stairs and went into Tavan's bedchamber. He sat in a chair and began to unlace his shoes. "'Tis time to move back upstairs."

Already in bed, Mackinzie asked, "You no longer fear a fire?"

"Nay, I believe 'tis safe now." He removed the rest of his clothing and climbed into bed beside her.

"I heard a wolf howling earlier."

"So did I. I shall send the lads out tomorrow to hunt them."

"Good. I care not to have them so close to the village." As soon as he reached for her, she moved closer and closed her eyes. "Why did you send all three of our sons to the Buchannans? I fear they will all be captured."

"I sent one to see about Kristin and two to see how to get her out. Samuel is a good lad, but he'll not be thinking straight."

"But suppose they *are* captured?"

Sawney kissed the top of her head. "My love, Laird Buchannan is not daft, although he pretends not to know the truth well enough. He is weakened and he does not wish to fight us. Instead, he will try to get the MacGraw to do it for him."

"How?"

"He will promise Kristin to Laird MacGraw, and then claim we have taken her."

"Then we must get her out before he can."

"Aye, hopefully our sons will manage to bring her back."

"But Laird Buchannan might still claim we have taken Kristin from him."

"Aye, but I sent word to Laird MacGraw not to believe it. And..."

"And what?" she asked.

"And not to attack the Buchannans until after we get her out."

"How clever you are. Will Laird MacGraw honor your wishes?"

"If he is wise."

Mackinzie listened to the beat of her husband's heart for a moment. "There will be a war after all, am I right?"

"I will do my best to avoid it." He was bone tired and needed rest, but his mind was full of all sorts of things that could go wrong. "I am not so certain my lads are willing to fight to get Kristin back. They will be, if the Buchannans try to keep my sons, but for Kristin alone..."

"They will do as you command, I know they will."

"Aye, but they will not like it and perhaps will not do their best. A lad who does not believe the cause is just, becomes slothful and endangers us all."

*

The next morning, Tavan went up to see Kristin. Samuel let Mary go home to sleep and managed to rest in a chair beside Kristin's bed for most of the night. He was happy to have the relief when Tavan came and quickly left.

Tavan sat in Samuel's chair and watched her. She looked a little better, but she was clearly not well enough to ride a horse home. He considered just holding her in his arms on his horse, but what if it killed her? That, he could never forgive himself for. She looked so helpless; the way Colina had the last time she got the fever. He did love Kristin; who wouldn't at a time like this?

"Tavan?"

He quickly sat up straight. "Forgive me, I drifted off."

"Has father gone home?"

"Nay, shall I fetch him?"

"Not yet. Is he well?"

"Did I not promise to watch over him?"

"Aye, you did. Tavan, my mother suffered here. I did not tell Father for it would deeply hurt him, but Arabella was hated by everyone. And Tavan, 'tis possible I have a sister, a brother or both living still."

"Where?"

"With the MacGreagors, I think."

He looked away. He liked intrigue as well as anyone and tried to think who might have acquired a child not their own. "I do not see how. She might have given them to another clan."

"Aye, 'tis possible. I should like having a sister or a brother."

"I shall like helping you find out." He wondered if she knew Gordon was her uncle and decided he did not want to be the one to tell her.

"Sawney would know."

"Aye, but my father is a master at keeping secrets. I will have to trick him into telling and 'tis not easy. Shall I begin the search right away or wait until you come home?"

"It must be our secret alone," said she.

"Agreed."

"Then I shall tell you this; Arabella insisted on a MacGreagor midwife."

Tavan sat back in his chair. He remembered Nonie saying she knew a secret about a midwife, and suspected he had just stumbled on to what it was. "You wish me to ask the midwife?"

"Who else would know?"

"Who else indeed."

"Do not wait. Ask as soon as you get home."

"I will. Kristin, we must go back or Father will think we are captured. Will you be alright?"

"Aye, Michael and Mary will see that I am. They do not know, I mean, I did not tell them Hendry's marriage to my mother was not true."

"There is much gossip. They will hear it soon anyway."

"I suppose I should tell them, then. There is more; Mary said Arabella was not Hendry's first wife. His first wife..." She had only just finished telling him when Mary knocked on the door and slipped inside. She peeked back out the door, looked up and down the hall, closed the door and then went to sit on the other side of Kristin's bed.

"Hendry does not intend to take her back," she whispered just loud enough for Tavan to hear.

"We know," he whispered back.

"What will you do?"

"I do not yet know. Samuel will insist we come after her and so will I."

"A war then. We lost half our lot in the last one. Our women have no husbands and their children, no fathers. I doubt we can survive another."

"Yet Hendry will fight to keep her?" Tavan asked.

"Aye, unless…" Mary paused and looked at Kristin.

"Go on," said Tavan.

"Unless you claim her."

"He thinks to marry her off?" Tavan asked.

"To Laird MacGraw, is Michael's guess. 'Tis a fate worse than poison. You are Laird MacGreagor's son. If you claim her and Laird MacGraw hears, he'll not risk a war with you."

"'Tis sound reasoning. How do we make certain Laird MacGraw hears?"

"If you agree, Michael will see he hears."

Tavan studied Mary's eyes for a long moment "Michael could die for betraying his laird."

"He will surely die if we go to war and I cannot live without him."

Tavan smiled. "I look forward to the kind of love you have for your husband."

"Tis the only thing worth living for. Will you agree?"

Tavan turned his attention to Kristin. "Hendry will try to talk you out of it. Can you manage?"

"I'd not like being married off against my will. I can manage it."

"Then we agree. I will announce it before we leave."

*

In the Buchannan great hall, Samuel was overjoyed, Callum and Patrick were perplexed and Laird Hendry Buchannan was clearly not pleased. "I see," Hendry said. He walked to a table, filled his goblet with wine and drank the whole thing down. Every lass needed the approval of her father and Kristin's father did not agree.

Tavan avoided looking at Michael, who stood quietly by listening. Tavan's only concern was Hendry's reaction. "I shall expect you to take her home as soon as she is well enough."

"I am certain you shall."

It was not a confirmation, so Tavan decided to press the matter. "Have I your pledge?"

Hendry filled his goblet a second time, set the pitcher down and finally turned around. "Aye."

"Good. I thank you for taking care of her and you as well Michael." Only then did he look at Michael. "Perhaps you and your wife might come with Laird Buchannan when he attends the wedding."

Michael nodded. "Just now I am reminded, you have my horse. I shall send a lad with you to fetch it."

Tavan returned Michael's nod, bowed to Laird Buchannan, walked to his brothers and as soon as they turned, he went out the door behind them. He was happy to be leaving, but not without Kristin and after he mounted his horse, he once more considered taking her home with him. For a moment, he looked up at the window on the third floor. It would be impossible to get her out of such a fortress without killing most of the Buchannans, which was not something he was looking forward to.

As if he knew what Tavan was thinking, Samuel said, "It would surely kill her."

"We could stop often," Tavan argued.

"It pains me to leave her as well, but it is too soon. You saw her, she is too feeble. Suppose moving her makes the poison go to her mind."

Tavan took a deep breath and slowly let it out. Then he turned his horse and walked it slowly across the courtyard and out through the double gates. As soon as the MacGreagors passed through, the gates began to close behind them. Tavan did not stop until they got to the top of the hill, then he halted his horse, turned around and looked back. It was, he suspected, what a man in love would do and for Hendry's sake, he had to make it look as real as possible.

*

On the way home, little was said in the company of the Buchannan and it was just as well. Tavan's head was swimming with what Kristin told him, and he was consumed with thoughts of how to discover if she had living siblings. He was as perplexed by how Arabella decided which to keep and which to give away, as Kristin was. That too, he hoped to discover. Most of all, he liked how Kristin trusted him and felt at ease telling him everything. Circumstances had made them trusted friends, but was the look in her eyes love? He could not be certain. Perhaps if she felt it, she was too sick to let it show. Yet before he left, he helped her sit up a little more. She put her arms around his neck, and he liked the way it felt very much. He held her a little longer than was necessary, but she did not object. Even so, did she see it as comfort and not love? Did he? There was definitely a lot left unsaid between them.

When they stopped to rest, Tavan stood at the edge of the pleasant pond, watching several swans dive down to nibble on vegetation below the surface of the water. For Michael's plan to work, he had to make all the MacGreagors believe he had truly claimed Kristin. Fooling his father would be the hardest, but if Sawney knew the truth, he would tell Mackinzie. As much as Tavan loved his mother, there was no guarantee Mackinzie would not let it slip.

Then there was Jenae.

*

Jenae tried not to watch for Tavan, but she couldn't seem to help herself. She worried that he was captured, or hurt and most of all, that he loved Kristin. It was enough to make her go daft, so she took her time doing chores and when she could bear it no longer, she mounted her horse and rode off to visit her uncle in the gardens. The fall leaves had never looked so beautiful, but her feeling of dread kept her from enjoying them. Even the calves and lambs brought her little joy, and she considered going back, but quickly changed her mind. She would know Tavan was home when Samuel came, and she would also know if they brought Kristin back. By the time she went home, everyone else would have finished greeting them and Tavan would be in the Keep, giving his report to Sawney. She couldn't avoid him forever, but a few more hours might help. Still, she missed him so much, her heart was hurting.

*

The whistles announced their arrival and as the returning

MacGreagors casually rode up the path in the middle of the glen, Tavan looked for Jenae. She was not there. Perhaps that was best. Sawney and the rest of the family came out of the Keep to greet them and Sawney's look of concern was unmistakable, so Patrick rode on ahead to ease his mind. Samuel split off and headed for home, just as a man brought Michael's horse for the young Buchanan boy to take back.

The first thing Tavan noticed when he rode into the courtyard, was Sharla standing near the door of the storehouse glaring at him. He smiled and nodded to her. He dismounted, let a boy lead his horse away and went to join his family in the great hall. He accepted the goblet of wine his sister handed him, took a drink to wash the dust out of his mouth and then took a deep breath. "Father, I have claimed Kristin."

"What?"

"I will take her to wife when she is back."

Sawney could not hide his true feelings and looked away. "Son, claiming her will not force Laird Buchannan to return her. A lad such as he does not care who he upsets."

"I know Father, but I love Kristin. Was it not you who said I should marry for love?"

"Does she love you?" Sawney asked.

"Aye."

Sawney shook his head, "'Twill not get her out."

"We could abduct her," Patrick suggested.

Tavan rolled his eyes. "How? You saw the fence, and she will not likely be going for a walk in the forest anytime soon. Michael's wife said she is unsteady on her feet. The poison has caused her great harm."

Callum pulled a chair out and sat down next to Patrick at the table. "She truly looks like death is at her door. Yet, neither her health nor her betrothal will keep Laird Buchannan from promising her to some other laird. Is that not what daughters are for?" He looked at the frown on his sister's face. "Colina, you would marry to prevent a war, would you not?"

She thought about that. "I would."

"And so will Kristin," Callum continued. "If we are to get her out, we best do it quickly."

"Get her out how?" Patrick asked. "I saw no stairs in the back. She has a window in her bedchamber and even if she managed to crawl out of it, 'tis three floors up."

"I could throw a rope to her and climb up to get her, I suppose," Tavan said. "She is not strong enough to climb a rope on her own."

"Even if she were, there are the gates still. How do we get them to open the gates?" Callum asked.

Patrick frowned. "We must start a fire in the back and force them out the front gates."

Mackinzie nearly choked on her sip of water. "Fire? Please...say you will not use fire."

"She is right," said Sawney. "Is there no other way?"

"I can think of no other," Patrick admitted. "Unless she manages to come out on her own, we are forced to go in and get her. Many will die...it cannot be helped."

Callum stroked his beard for a moment. "I was not pleased with

the look on Laird Buchannan's face when Tavan claimed her. If I were
he, I would use Kristin to prevent a second battle with the MacGraw.
Now, he just might do it sooner than he planned."

Tavan had not considered that. Still, Michael might be able to
prevent it, at least until Kristin was well enough to be brought home.
"Let him betroth her to fifty lads, she will not agree to marry until she
is well. She will stall for time."

"I hope you are right," Sawney muttered.

"How much time?" Patrick asked.

"Another week, perhaps," Tavan answered.

"Perhaps no more than a week," Callum said, "and we've got the
harvest festival tomorrow. Our lads will not want to fight until after."

"If they will fight at all," Sawney said.

Tavan looked puzzled, "They will not fight to save a
MacGreagor?"

"'Tis different with Kristin," said Sawney.

"How so?" Tavan asked, his ire already beginning to rise.

"Son, she is Arabella's daughter." As soon as he said it, Sawney
regretted his remark. Tavan could do nothing less than defend Kristin
now. "Forgive me, I did not mean…"

Tavan stood up and started for the door. "I know what you meant,
Father."

CHAPTER X

Just as Jenae suspected, when she got home Tavan was inside the Keep and probably would be the rest of the day. According to her friends, they did not bring Kristin back. It looked like it might rain again, but she approved. The gloomy feeling in her heart exactly matched the gloomy sky. She was nearly to the cottage she shared with her father when Tavan walked up the path toward her.

Tavan thought it was best not to see or speak to Jenae again, if he could avoid it, yet when he noticed her, not speaking seemed too unkind. He stopped. "Are you well? I mean, is all well with you now that Father makes Sharla open the storehouse door."

She couldn't help but grin. "I have never seen her this enraged."

"She deserves it, and more."

"How is Kristin?"

"Not well, but she will live. Jenae, I have claimed Kristin and she has agreed." What he saw in Jenae's eyes was a kind of sadness he was not at all prepared for. It was hard for him to look at and when she didn't look away, he finally had to. "I must go."

"You love her?"

Suddenly, he knew which woman was truly in his heart - it was Jenae. He tried hard not to let the truth show, but he hadn't counted on how hard it would be to lie to her. "Aye." He felt like the worst kind of rogue in the world. He let Jenae think he cared for her; he let the whole clan think he cared for her, and now she was forced to live with his rejection. He wanted to wrap his arms around her and tell her the truth, but he reminded himself it was to free a MacGreagor.

She forced a smile. "Then I approve. If I had a sister, I would wish her to be just like Kristin. I used to dream of it when we were children and the truth be told, I would like it still."

"Even though she is Arabella's daughter?"

"'Tis an awful thing they say about Arabella." Jenae started to walk down the path and was pleased when Tavan walked with her. "It cannot all be true. When she came, Arabella always ran into Samuel's arms. Of course, everyone save Kristin knew she was his wife. Once, Arabella caught Samuel off balance and knocked him down. I shall never forget how they lay on the ground together laughing so hard I feared they would hurt themselves."

Jenae glanced at the perplexed look on Tavan's face. "So you see, I cannot believe she was so very awful. True, she left him for another, but she kept coming back to him, not just to see her daughter, but to be with Samuel. She still loved him, I think."

"The more I hear about Arabella, the more I am confounded. Perhaps she loved them both?"

"She must have. I wish to see Kristin, will you take me to her?"

People were watching and he dared not stay with her any longer. "'Tis not safe." He could tell she was trying hard not to let her feelings show, but the sadness was still in her eyes. "Jenae, I am sorry…"

"Nay, 'tis I who begs forgiveness. I should not have placed that wager with Sharla; it was a childish thing to do." She smiled, nodded and headed back toward her cottage.

What she wanted to do most was to find a place to be alone and cry, so she took the path to the loch instead. Then she remembered the men bathed in the evening and quickly turned down another path. At last, she found a rock to sit on in the forest and released her tears.

She felt almost as bad as she did the day her mother did not wake up. Tavan never favored her, she could see that now. How was she ever to face anyone again? Even her father commented on how attentive he was to her during the harvest, and the clan would soon look on her with great pity -- all except Sharla, who was bound to be very pleased.

It all seemed too cruel and it made Jenae's tears turn to sobs. What she needed most was to get away for a while. Far, far away where no one knew Tavan had rejected her. An idea was forming in her mind and it was almost dark by the time she pulled herself together and went home.

*

At last, Tavan lay down in his bed and closed his eyes. Callum was right, Hendry might marry Kristin off before they could rescue her, and she would agree if she thought it would prevent a war. His only hope was that Michael could get word to Laird MacGraw in time, and that the MacGraws would not be willing to fight the MacGreagors for her.

Most of all, he thought about Jenae. She took the news so graciously and even found a reason why he had rejected her, which if true, would have made him feel much better. In truth, he'd forgotten all about her wager with Sharla, and did not hold it against her. All he could do now was pray his plan to free Kristin would work and that someday soon, he could tell Jenae, that is, if he wasn't forced to actually marry Kristin to save her.

*

Morning brought an early bustle of activity to the MacGreagor glen. There were games to prepare, food to make ready, tables and chairs to bring out, and fresh bread to bake in the stone kilns. The air was filled with the magnificent aroma of smoked beef and well-cooked ham in the pits. As soon as the milking was done, the farmers arrived in the glen, some bringing extra barrel churns so the women could make the milk into sweet cream and butter.

Appetites could hardly wait for the serving to begin and none anticipated it more than Tavan. Yet he hungered for more than food -- he wanted information. He filled his bowl with all sorts of delights, and intentionally sought out the one woman he thought would have all the answers - Jernoot, the same midwife who helped his mother bring her triplets into the world.

The years had been good to Jernoot, although her hair was gray and her stature a little more stooped than it once was. She sat in a chair near the Keep, and needed only to look around to see all the people she helped bring into the world. Some women had an easy birth, but there were also complications such as a breach, a baby that did not draw breath and occasionally, a mother who's bleeding could not be stopped. Yet Jernoot was proud to know more mothers and babies lived than died. It was her plight in life and she was happy to help, although there were nights she would rather have been in bed.

She hardly noticed Tavan when he sat in the chair beside her. Instead, she watched the chatting, laughing people and savored the taste of each morsel of ham she put in her mouth. Never did a meal taste so good as salted ham at a harvest festival.

"Jernoot," Tavan began. "Do you know all their names?"

"Of course I do, though I wager you do not."

"'Tis a wager you would win. What do you suppose is the matter with me?"

"You are lazy, Tavan MacGreagor."

Tavan's mouth dropped. "Lazy?"

"Aye, you were likely the last born and as I recall, the last wanted no part of leaving the comfort of his mother's womb. I have decided you were the last."

"Good, then I shall not be named the next laird. Pray do tell everyone you see."

Jernoot giggled. "I already have." She was surprised and a little embarrassed when he put an arm around her and kissed her cheek.

"Thank you," he said. "You are right, I suspect I am too lazy to learn all their names." He took a long, slow look at the many faces, hoping he could tell if any resembled Kristin, but he could not. "Tell me, which are Arabella's children?"

Jernoot caught her breath and quickly looked around to make certain no one was paying any attention to them. "How...I mean, where...who said there were others?"

"The Buchannans."

She closed her eyes for a moment. "Do not pursue this, Tavan. 'Twould be too unkind to a child who does not suspect."

"Kristin wishes to know."

"Kristin had not yet tasted the wrath of those who hated Arabella.

Once she is aware, she'll not wish the others exposed any more than I do. Please do not ask, I cannot tell you."

"Then tell me this -- how did Arabella choose which to keep?"

"She kept only her sons." As soon as she noticed Patrick coming toward them, she grabbed Tavan's hand and squeezed it. "Hush now, lad."

He stood up, leaned down and kissed the top of her head. "I did not mean to upset you."

"What have you done this time?" Patrick wanted to know.

"Brother, have you no wife and child to tend?" Tavan shot back. He left Jernoot, walked to a table filled with breads and chose a piece with various kinds of seeds in it. Thankfully, Patrick followed instead of questioning Jernoot.

"My wife prefers to eat with Kylie, who enjoys the company of Callum...for a reason I do not understand," said Patrick.

"Perhaps Kylie loves Callum."

"And why not, he looks just like us." Intentionally, Patrick took hold of Tavan's elbow and steered him to the edge of the crowd where they could talk. "Where is Jenae?"

"How am I to know?"

"Brother, you may have fooled the rest of them, but not me. 'Tis Jenae you love, not Kristin."

Tavan would have given half his life to confide in someone, but the risk was too high. "The truth be told, you do not want me to love Kristin. Marriage to her would complicate all our lives and you would rather it not."

"How little you know of me. I would welcome Kristin as eagerly as Jenae, but Kristin is not the one in your heart. Deny it if you can, but do you not look for Jenae? Have you not been looking for her all morning?"

"I look for her, because…I have hurt her."

"Hurt her how?"

"I believe she expected me to choose her and the fault is mine. I let her think I felt more for her than I do. I only wish to know she is… she is not unwell, is she?"

"If I said she was, you would go daft with worry. Nay, she is fine. She has gone to see a new calf born last night. 'Tis late in the year for a birth and she wished to see for herself that it will survive."

"You have seen her?"

"There, you see, you do love her."

Tavan rolled his eyes and walked away.

*

While the MacGreagors feasted on beef and pork at their harvest festival, Hendry carried Kristin outside, set her in a chair and made certain she was warm enough. Their traditional festival was not so very different. This time, when Kristin met the people, they were far more friendly. Children brought her flowers and Mary filled her bowl with far more than she could manage to eat. Afterwards, two stout men lifted her, chair and all, and carried her through the gates so she could watch the activities.

First, several boys who could not have been more than five or six, raced on foot with all the determination they could muster for the cheering crowd. Kristin rewarded the winner with a kiss on the cheek, which he promptly wiped off. Next came the handoff races with two teams of men running up the hill and down again, handing a goblet from one to another. The object, she learned, was not to spill all the water out of the goblet. Both goblets were bone dry when the teams returned and the crowd roared with laughter. After that, the men held an ordinary foot race.

The races on horseback were the most impressive and exciting. Part of the course was out of her sight, but Kristin could hear cheers from the clan each time the men rounded a specific marker. Then they raced down the hill, with the first three seemingly neck and neck, until two managed to pull ahead. In the end, the race was declared a tie, much to the chagrin of the winners. Kristin had no doubt it would be the subject of many a discussion for months.

No sooner had the crowd calmed, than they became completely silent. Several children stood in front of Kristin and it took a moment for her to get them to move aside so she could see. To her amazement, a MacGreagor woman sat her horse on the top of the hill looking down on them.

*

It was, by far, the most terrifying and foolhardy thing Jenae had ever done, but that morning, she rode off to see her uncle in the gardens, turned when she was certain no one was watching and disappeared into the forest. She'd never been to the Buchannan village before, or even to the Haldane for that matter, and nearly got lost twice. Then she had to quickly hide in the trees when she heard the galloping racers coming her way. Literally shaking all over, she finally decided the coast was clear and showed herself. Now, all that was left was to ride into the Buchannan village and see what would happen.

The MacGreagor woman got quite close before Kristin recognized who she was and smiled. She watched Jenae dismount and then watched the Buchannans part so Jenae could come to her. Kristin put her hands on her hips and tried to look upset. "What have you done, Jenae?"

"I have escaped, finally," Jenae answered loud enough for all to hear. She was horrified by the way Kristin looked, but she tried not to show it as she hugged her friend "I have fretted so, are you very ill still?"

"I have seen better days." When Hendry came to her, Kristin said, "Jenae, this is my other father. I call him Hendry, but he prefers Laird Buchannan."

"Ah, but if she is your friend," he said, "Hendry will do." He was pleased when Jenae curtsied to him as he felt she should. "Am I to expect a hundred MacGreagors to come?"

"Not for a day or two. I have come to rescue Kristin, if she is well enough. If not, I intend to stay until she is."

Hendry smiled. He hardly thought the little slip of a girl could rescue anyone, but he admired her courage. "Tell me true, did Laird MacGreagor send you to spy on me?"

"Of course. He uses all the lasses as spies, those not with child that is." She put her nose in the air ever so slightly. "'Tis very fair of him, I think. Now, what secrets have you for me to discover?"

Hendry laughed. He liked her; she had Kristin's same tenacity. Perhaps all MacGreagor women were like that. He noticed Kristin looked at Jenae with fondness and Michael seemed to be enjoying the conversation very much. Mary had not left Kristin's side and for a moment, he envied the loyalty they seemed to have for his daughter.

Each day, there were new reasons not to marry Kristin off as he intended. The clan was learning to love Arabella's daughter and he didn't blame them. They might not be happy if he married her off, but he could not think of another way to pacify Laird MacGraw. Just this morning, his spies reported the MacGraw looked like they were preparing for another battle. Soon after, Hendry sent a man with a message hinting that he might be willing to exchange his daughter for peace between them, but it was too soon to expect a reply.

Then there were the MacGreagors. Would his men be willing to fight to keep her if the MacGreagors came before the MacGraw attacked? Perhaps so. If by chance they beat the MacGreagors, then he could use Kristin to pacify Laird MacGraw. Yes, it was the perfect plan, he decided -- if they could keep the MacGreagors from taking Kristin.

"Are you hungry?" Kristin asked Jenae.

"Starved."

One of the men brought another chair, smiled at her a little too long, and made both Jenae and Kristin giggle after he put it down and walked away. Between bites of bread, chicken and cheese, Jenae told Kristin what Tavan had done to Sharla. The way she told it was delightful and captivated everyone nearby. Even Hendry was intrigued. Then she answered all of Kristin's questions about the harvest and Samuel. She neglected to report her mother's death, but that could wait.

Kristin smiled repeatedly, but Jenae mentioned Tavan far too often and there was no doubt in Kristin's mind, that Jenae was madly in love with the man she was supposed to be marrying. "Did he tell you we are to wed?"

"Aye, he told everyone and happily so. Tavan loves you and I am certain you can manage him very well indeed."

"I shall try," said Kristin.

It was harder to pretend being happy for Kristin than Jenae thought, but she was certain she was doing very well at keeping her feelings concealed. "You do love him, I can tell."

"Of course I do, I'd not marry him otherwise," said Kristin.

"Then I am very happy for you. Now, how long before I can snatch you away and take you home to him?"

*

The day the triplets and Samuel left, Michael sent a man to tell Laird MacGraw Kristin was promised, but the man had not yet returned and Michael was worried. Did Hendry suspect and had he captured the man Michael sent? There seemed no hint of animosity in Hendry's manner, but Hendry was very good at hiding his true feelings.

Just now however, Michael was more concerned about Kristin. "You are tired. Allow me to take you back inside where it is warmer." He was glad she agreed, picked her up and carried her back inside the Keep. Once there, he asked, "Shall I take you up to bed now?"

"Aye."

With Jenae and Mary following, Michael crossed the room and started up the stairs

*

Dancing to the music of the flute player was a favorite of all clans and the Buchannans were no different, although flute players were sometimes scarce. Hendry watched, but his mind was on other things. Not for a moment, did he think Jenae came alone and after she arrived, he sent guards to scour the woods. They found no one and he could think of no reason Sawney would allow her to come alone. Perhaps she had a guard, and once she was delivered, they went back. Or...Sawney didn't know she had come.

If Sawney didn't know, that opened up a whole new set of problems. The MacGreagors might not attack to get one woman back, but they would, now that there were two.

*

Finally back in bed and with Jenae in a chair nearby, Kristin relaxed and closed her eyes for a moment. It was true she and Jenae played together as children, and she was probably closer to her than any other young women, yet what Jenae was doing went far beyond friendship.

Kristin opened her eyes and studied Jenae's features. There was a slight resemblance, but not to Arabella...to Samuel. It was possible Samuel fathered a child Arabella gave away. If Arabella knew it was Samuel's child, perhaps she wanted her daughter to be raised by the MacGreagors. Still, why not give them both to Samuel? Perhaps the midwife made the decision. In any case, did Jenae know? Did she come because they truly were sisters? The thought both thrilled and upset Kristin. One thing was for sure, she would never tell Hendry there were other children for him to claim.

*

Unlike the dancing, the laughter, the music and the fun in the

Buchannan village, there was little more than a soft muttering of voices in the courtyard of the MacGreagors.

"I intend to go get Kristin and bring her home," said Sawney." He had their attention, but he was not pleased with their reaction.

"You'll go without me," Gordon shouted. "I'll not give my blood for the likes of Kristin."

Sawney put his hand on Tavan's shoulder and climbed up so he could stand on the short stonewall. "Does he speak for all of you?" He expected yeas or nays, but his question was met with more whispers. "She is a MacGreagor. Dare we let more harm to come to her?"

Gordon pushed his way to the front of the crowd. "She is Arabella's daughter, if we bring her back, the harm will come *from* her, not *to* her."

"'Tis in her blood," said a woman in the back.

Gordon vigorously nodded, "Aye, 'tis in Kristin's blood, just like her mother and her mother before her."

"I'll hear no more of this!" Samuel shouted. "She is my daughter, and if I must, I shall go alone to fight for her."

"As will I," said Tavan.

Dollag, Sharla's mother, pushed her way through the crowd too. "'Only the daft would marry her. Look what her mother did to Samuel."

Sile's voice was loud, clear and without a hint of a stammer when she shouted, "'Tis in her blood, you say?"

Gordon's shout was just a clear, "Be still, old lass, everyone knows you are feeble minded."

Furious and emboldened for the first time in years, she did not look away from Gordon's accusing eyes. "Tavan, lift me up on the wall, I've something to say."

Tavan did as she asked, and soon, little Sile towered over everyone. She was so angry, she did not notice when Sawney put his arm around her to her make certain she would not fall. "Let no voice be heard save yours, Gordon? But you and I know a truth."

"I warn you, Sile, do not say it." Gordon forgot himself and before he knew it, all three of the triplets moved to stand between him and Sile.

Sawney raised his hand to quiet the mumbling crowd. "I will hear what Sile has to say."

Sile drew in a deep breath. "They all know you are Arabella's brother, Gordon. They have known it for days."

She watched him bow his head, finally took her eyes off of Gordon and looked at Samuel. "How often over the years did I come to you, Samuel? Did you think I came because I fancied you? I tell you true, I could never favor a lad as stupid as you."

Samuel drew back at her insult. "Stupid?"

"Aye, you heard it right. 'Twas Arabella who sent me."

"You knew her?" Samuel asked.

"Best of us all, I knew her." She thought she might cry, so Sile took another deep breath. "Not once did Arabella slight me for my stammer, which is more than I can say for many here." She glared at a few of the women and made them look away. "Samuel MacGreagor, how could you not see what truly happened? One day she loved you beyond the stars and the next she did not? How easily you let her walk away. You believed what they said, you expected it, and when she left, you thought she could not help it - adultery was in her blood."

"I…" Samuel muttered.

"Buchannan forced her!" Sile wanted to laugh at the shock on Samuel's face. "MacGreagors are vowed to kill for such a thing and you would have called him out. She could not lose you…any of you, so she did not tell."

"She should not have walked the forest alone," Gordon said. "She brought it upon herself."

"Show me a lass who does not go into the forest alone." Sile waited, but no one spoke. Again, she addressed Samuel. "Arabella could not live with you, and could not abide living with him. Where was she to be, save in the forest? She knew what was said of her. Shall I tell which lads sought her out, for Arabella often hid me behind a bush when they came?

It was exactly what Sawney feared would happen and he held his breath. A few of the men widened their eyes and some of the wives noticed. "Nay Sile, 'twould do no good now," Sawney whispered.

Still fuming mad, Sile would like nothing better than to name them, but she honored Sawney's request. "Arabella cried for the shame she carried. No MacGreagor lass cared what happened to her. After Kristin was born, she knew not how to bind her breasts so her milk would not come in. When I found her, she was in agony."

Dollag was not the least bit sorry for Arabella. "Why would we care, she was a temptress. Gordon is right, 'Twas in her blood"

"Tell me, whose blood do we blame for the lads who forced her?" Sile shouted.

Samuel didn't care about all that just now. "If she loved me, how could she leave me?"

"Still you do not see? Buchannan thought to free her by killing you. She lied to keep *you* alive, *you*, Samuel MacGreagor. No lass ever loved a lad more than she loved you."

Samuel closed his eyes and slowly bowed his head.

"She abandoned her own child. What lass does that?" Dollag shouted.

"A lass who did not want her daughter to carry the scar of Murdina's blood...yet you say it still. Do you think Murdina had only one daughter? You do not say it of me, and I am Arabella's sister."

"Your stammer is her curse upon you," Gordon said.

"Your hate is far worse than my stammer."

A woman shouted, "Who killed Murdina?"

"I do not know, nor did Arabella," Sile answered.

"Which MacGreagor lads forced Arabella?" another woman demanded to know.

Sile did not mean to answer, but it just slipped out, "Ainsley for one."

"Nay, 'tis not true. Ainsley loved me!" Dollag shouted, tears beginning to form in her eyes. "'Tis a lie!"

'Tis not a lie. Did Arabella not give you Ainsley's daughter? Was that not how you knew what he had done?" She paused for a moment. "It was you who set him on fire, I saw you do it."

Sharla's mother sank to her knees. "I had to kill him, I could not let him live."

Shocked, Sharla stared at her weeping mother and then turned to Sile. "I am *not* Arabella's daughter, I hate the forest."

Just then, Jenae's father raced his horse into the glen, dismounted and ran to Sawney. "Jenae is gone. She went to the gardens to see her uncle this morning, but she never arrived.'

"Oh no," Tavan muttered. "She has gone to see Kristin."

"What?" Sawney asked.

"She asked me to take her to see Kristin and I refused."

Sawney held up his hand once more to silence the mumbling clan. "At dawn I shall ride to the Buchannan village and collect what is mine. Who is with me?" He was pleased when all the men said, "Aye," all except Gordon who quietly walked out of the courtyard. "See to your rest lads, we leave tomorrow at first light."

There was little to be joyful about when the people dispersed and went about the preparations. With tears in their eyes, the women cleared away what was left of the feast. The older boys carried tables and chairs back to cottages, while the men began to sharpen daggers, swords and the tips of arrows. There were flasks to fill, bandages to prepare, and horses hooves to check. Only then would they hold their loved ones in their arms, for perhaps the last time.

*

It was nearly dusk when someone knocked on Sile's door. It had been a tiring day and Sile would rather everyone left her alone, but she begrudgingly answered the knock anyway. To her surprise, Samuel stood there with his eyes cast down. He seemed to have something to say, but could not find the words. She was about to close her door in his face, when he reached out and stopped her.

"I have come…to beg forgiveness."

She couldn't seem to keep the tears from rolling down her cheeks and when he opened his arms, she gladly went into them.

*

Later that morning, Hendry Buchannan was worried. He still had not heard anything from laird MacGraw. Was his offer of a wife not good enough? What more could MacGraw want? Worse still, none of his guards reported in that morning, which could only mean one thing - either the MacGraws or the MacGreagors captured them.

He ran his fingers through his hair and looked at the man standing in front of him. "The MacGraw will burn us out, the MacGreagors will not, not as long as Kristin and Jenae are within."

"Then we must pray they are MacGreagors," Michael said.

"We must pray the MacGreagors and the MacGraw have not banded together. We might survive one, but not both."

"Perhaps you should give the lasses up."

"Not Kristin, I shall never give her up."

"You are out of your wits," Michael said. "We are not strong enough to defeat the MacGreagors or the MacGraw, and you well know it."

"You dare argue with me, Michael?"

"I dare try to save the life of my wife and son. You have lost, Hendry. Do not make the rest of us pay for it."

Jenae sat on the second from the top stair step and peeked through a hole in the wooden banister. She'd heard enough, eased back up to the top step and went to tell Kristin. Yet once she got to Kristin's bedchamber, she changed her mind. Kristin as awake, but she looked too tired to hear bad news. Let her rest peacefully, Jenae thought. It was the first time she noticed the carved horse on Kristin's table and her heart sank. Tavan truly did love Kristin and the horse he carved was the proof. She took a moment to look at the jeweled goblet atop a trunk and pulled herself together. "Tis a very grand castle you live in, me lady," Jenae teased.

Kristin giggled, "No finer in all of Scotland."

"Perhaps while you sleep, I shall see to our escape."

Again Kristin giggle, "Oh yes, please do. I long to walk all the way home."

"Fear not, when you tire, I shall carry you on my back."

Kristin yawned, smiled and closed her eyes. "Thank you. You are the dearest friend in all the world."

Jenae waited until she thought Kristin was asleep and then quietly left the room. There was much to explore and if there was another way out besides the great hall, she intended to find it. Quietly, she opened door after door on that level and then climbed the stone stairs up to the next.

*

Tavan rode behind his father in the middle of no less than four hundred warriors. As soon as he heard Jenae was gone, he became frantic. The thought of her in the arms of a Buchannan was nearly driving him mad. He watched for her along the way, just in case her horse threw her, but he saw nothing.

A little more than halfway there, the MacGreagors began to scour the woods and capture Buchannan lookouts. It was far easier done than Sawney anticipated and he was certain Hendry would have little forewarning, if any.

Quietly riding beside Sawney, Samuel looked to be suffering even more than the day he heard his wife was dead. It wasn't hard to figure out why. At last, Sawney could bear it no longer. "I believed it too."

"What?" Samuel asked.

"That Arabella was willing."

Samuel drew in a deep breath and shook his head. "How shall I ever forgive myself?"

"She should have told us, we would have killed Buchannan for what he did."

"You heard Sile. She did not want any to die."

"There are many ways to kill a lad short of war. I wonder that she didn't tell me, at least."

"You were very young, newly married and...and I thank you, but the fault is mine. I could not see beyond my anger. I think now about the times she came, and still I did not see the love she had for me. Sile is right, I am stupid."

"Sile says the same to me."

Samuel almost smiled. "She calls you stupid?"

"She is the only one brave enough. Would that I had a hundred warriors as bold as Sile."

"Sawney, I wish to kill Buchannan myself."

"You would lose."

"I should have done it in the beginning."

"You would have lost then too." They were getting closer and when Samuel began to speak again, Sawney quieted him. He kept his eyes on the man in the lead and when he raised his hand, Sawney motioned for all the men to halt their horses.

"'Tis just over the next hill," Tavan said as he drew his horse closer to his father's. "The path widens into a glen and beyond that are the gates." Tavan pulled his horse back a little and waited. In the distance, the two men in the lead quietly walked their horses into the trees, and started up the hill to have a look around. Endless moments passed before they returned and one made his way to Sawney.

"They have piled their weapons in the middle of the glen."

"The lads?" Sawney asked.

"They sit to one side in the grass unarmed and waiting."

Sawney frowned. "They were warned. We missed a guard or two."

"Nay, they saw us coming from the guard towers," said the warrior.

"Tis a trap," Samuel whispered.

"Aye," Sawney agreed. "Dismount."

They did at they were told, set their horses free, drew their swords and fell in behind Sawney. Step by step, they walked up the last hill and then stopped. Just as reported, the Buchannan warriors were sitting in the glen unarmed, watching them. Sawney paused to think for a moment.

"They refuse to fight for her," Tavan said.

"They know they cannot win," said Patrick.

Callum disagreed. "They will run for their weapons when we draw near."

"Perhaps," said Sawney. "We shall soon see. He raised his hand and motioned his men forward.

They were a force to be reckoned with, these large men of might with swords drawn and fierceness in their expression like no other, glaring and daring the Buchannans to move a muscle. Closer and closer they came, yet they heard no one shout a battle cry, saw no hint of aggression and felt no urgent sense of alarm.

Fearing an attack from behind, Sawney motioned for his warriors to guard the Buchannans and as soon as he felt it was safe, he, his sons and Samuel continued to walk toward the open double gates.

*

She had no idea how long she'd slept and wondered why she wasn't getting better. "Jenae," Kristin whispered, "I thirst." When no one answered, she forced her eyes open and looked around. She was alone, but thankfully someone had left a goblet on the table next to her. She struggled to sit up, took hold of the goblet, grasped it with both hands, lifted it to her mouth and drank. It tasted like spoiled wine, but at least it was wet. She put the goblet back and exchanged it for the horse Tavan gave her. She had it in her hand and had only just started to lie back when the room began to spin. The darkness quickly began to flood her eyes, and when she realized what was happening, she reached out her hand. "Jenae?"

*

Except for the crackling fire in the hearths, it was quiet in the Buchannan great hall -- too quiet. Hendry had nearly worn himself out pacing back and forth, trying to think what to do. He still had time, for no one had come to tell him danger was near. He had drunk more than his share of wine, but it was doing little to dull his apprehension. Michael should have come back by now, but he decided to give his faithful friend a little more time to find Myra.

It was late the night before when he remembered his first wife had a sister. How could he have forgotten about Myra, and why hadn't he guessed it was Myra who fed poison to his family? He closed his eyes for a moment. How clever of her to get help for Kristin so no doubt would befall on her. She must have thought it was too late to save Kristin.

It was true, Padrig confessed, but most likely to protect Myra. Padrig was dead and the Buchannans were better for it, but what was he to do about Myra? He supposed he would have to execute her too, but he hated the sight of death. Perhaps he could order Michael to do it again this time.

He thought about Arabella and how he loved having her in his arms, and in his bed. Sometimes she tried to forbid him, but it was just a game they played. Lately however, he'd been having second thoughts about her. If she loved him, how could she give his child away? It was unthinkable, but then, believing Arabella did not love him was also unthinkable. She stayed, didn't she?

Hendry couldn't think about that just now, turned toward the door and abruptly shouted, "Michael!"

*

Tavan looked for Michael among the Buchannan warriors, but he was not there. The trap might well be just inside the fence, but there was only one way to find out. Cautiously, he stepped just inside the gates and looked both directions. The women and children were gone and not one warrior showed himself, not even Michael. Tavan looked up at the guard towers in case the Buchannans thought to rain down arrows upon them, but he could see no one. He motioned for the archers to come forward, and waited for them to take up positions, kneel down and prepare to fire.

"Michael!" He heard Hendry bellow from inside.

Unarmed, Michael dared to peek round the side of the Keep and then quickly jerked his head back. He recognized Sawney in the middle and now, he had to pray the MacGreagor archers would not shoot him when he showed himself. Mustering all his courage, he stepped away from the building and held his hands out to show he had no weapons. Slowly, he walked to the center of the courtyard to face Sawney.

"Michael, I order you to come at once!" Hendry shouted again.

Michael rolled his eyes, glanced back and then faced Sawney again. "He is drunk."

"Where are Kristin and Jenae?" Tavan asked.

"Upstairs…"

Hendry abruptly jerked the door open and stepped out. "Mich…" His mouth dropped and he started to reach for his sword, but one of the archers turned toward him and he knew it would be useless. He gathered his wits as best he could and glared at Sawney. "She is not well enough yet. Did I not say I would bring her home?"

Suddenly, a woman upstairs screamed.

"Jenae," Tavan breathed. He ran past Hendry into the Keep with Jenae's father right behind him. He raced across the great hall and taking three at a time, Tavan flew up the stairs. He ran down the hall, up the second flight and abruptly stopped. Jenae stood in the hall with her back against the wall and her hand over her mouth, staring into Kristin's bedchamber. Her eyes were wild and a steady stream of tears ran down both her cheeks.

Terrified of what he was about to see, Tavan put his sword away and slowly went in. Jenae's father put his arms around her and together they watched Tavan.

Once he could see her face, Tavan couldn't seem to make his feet move. He found it impossible to fully grasp what had happened. The light was gone from her open eyes and it appeared Kristin was reaching out to someone. She was dead, he finally realized and at length, Tavan made himself move closer. He could not just leave her there. Tenderly, he closed her eyes, moved the covers away and put his arms under her. As if he feared hurting her, he gently drew her body to him. When he did, the carved horse fell out of her hand and landed on the wooden floor.

For a long moment, Tavan held her close and rocked her in his arms. Then at last, he turned to take her down to Samuel. "I will take her home now," he said, as he paused in front of Jenae. He waited for her tearful nod, and then started down the hallway.

*

They should have, but no one quite expected Samuel to turn as soon as he saw Kristin's body, screech his fury and run forward. With one swift movement, he thrust his sword completely through Hendry's torso. "You killed her, you killed them both!"

A disbelieving Hendry slumped to his knees.

Samuel put his foot on Hendry's chest and with rage still in his eyes, slowly and painfully withdrew his sword. "Die, Hendry Buchannan, die! May your soul feel the fires of hell for all eternity."

Hendry Buchannan passed before he heard the last of Samuel's curse. As soon as Samuel removed his foot, he fell forward and landed in a pool of his own blood.

It was finished.

The wickedness falsely put upon Arabella was finally absolved with the death of the man she hated. Even so, it cost the life of her beloved daughter and somewhere above, the angels wept.

The MacGreagors called for their horses, and the Buchannans bowed their heads as they watched Tavan carry Kristin into the glen and lay her down. Sawney helped Samuel wrap Kristin in a MacGreagor plaid, and together they tied her body over Jenae's horse. Then Sawney handed the reins to Tavan.

Jenae was so distraught, Sawney held her for a moment, kissed the top of her head and then lifted her into her father's arms. The last to mount his horse, Sawney turned and led the mournful funeral procession home.

When Tavan looked back, Michael was holding his crying wife in his arms and Hendry still lay in front of the Buchannan keep unattended.

CHAPTER XI

Kristin's body was washed, dressed in the clothing of her clan and laid out on the table in the MacGreagor great hall for all to see. Everyone came but Sharla, her mother and Gordon.

During the two days of mourning, Sawney sought to keep Tavan busy and sent all three of his sons off to accomplish a task he'd been carefully considering. When the triplets returned and Tavan nodded, he told Alec to fetch Gordon, Sharla and her mother.

He stood beside Kristin's body when he spoke and try as they might, each were forced to look at her remains. "For the killing of Ainsley," he began, "I banish you, Dollag. You may take Sharla with you or leave her with us."

"Banished? But where can I go?" Dollag whined.

"The MacDuff have agreed to take you in."

Sharla narrowed her eyes. "Tis just as well, I do not wish to be a MacGreagor."

"It is settled then. Gather your belongings and make ready."

Gordon knew what was coming, "And me? What shall you do with me?"

"For refusing to fight, you too shall be banished. Fortunately, you have no family and none will be hurt...unless you have finally decided to claim Sile as your sister."

"I have no sister," the hate-filled Gordon grumbled.

"Tell me, Gordon, what happened to your mother?"

He turned and headed for the door. "You shall never know."

*

Jenae's Father fully intended to punish her for running off, but she was so upset over the death of Kristin, he decided she had suffered enough. Together, they waited with the others for Tavan to return from taking Sharla and her mother to the MacDuff, then they fell in behind him, Sile and Samuel, to walk to the graveyard behind the strong men carrying Kristin's box.

Fast approaching storm clouds began to gather and once more, Jenae felt it fitting for such an awful occasion. She blamed herself for leaving Kristin alone that day and was certain she would never get over it. Still, she doubted she hurt nearly as much as Tavan, and if he could be strong, then she must be also. As soon as the priest finished the service, the rain appropriately began to fall and everyone quietly went home…all but Jenae.

She watched the grave diggers toss shovels full of dirt into the open grave, and just let the rain drench her, as if it could somehow wash away her awful sorrow. Not two feet away, was the grave of her mother.

Had she looked, she would have seen Tavan standing in the rain as well watching her, but she did not look.

*

The next day, Tavan took up carving again, sat in his favorite chair beside the hearth, and seemed to take more deep breaths, than he truly needed, Sawney thought. He was worried about his son, but there was little he could do. Mackinzie sat not far away tending some mending that most likely did not need to be done. Apparently, she couldn't think of anything to say either, that had not already been said.

At last, Tavan broke the silence. "Mother, how long should I wait to ask Jenae to marry me?"

"What?" Sawney said, quickly turning in his chair at the table.

Mackinzie smiled. "You have tricked us, I see."

Sawney couldn't help but get up and walk to the hearth. "You loved her all along?"

"Aye. Michael thought if Kristin and I were betrothed, Hendry could not betroth her to another. He sent word to Laird MacGraw warning him."

"As did I," Sawney admitted.

Tavan smiled. "I should have guessed that." He carefully set his carving down. "I have hurt Jenae, and badly. I wish nothing more than to relieve her suffering, now that…Kristin is gone."

"I agree," said Mackinzie. "I do not gossip, as you are well aware, but I shall make an exception for this occasion. Before the night is done, everyone will know you and Kristin were not truly betrothed."

Tavan shared a knowing look with his father, "Thank you, Mother, I was hoping you would. I best go tell Jenae before she hears it from others."

"You truly loved her all along?" Sawney asked.

"You did not suspect?"

"Well, I…" Before he could finish, Tavan was out the door.

*

There was an autumn chill in the air when Tavan found her and sat down next to Jenae on the large rock beside the river. The sun cast its sparkling reflection across the crisp, clear water, the birds chirped in the trees and the air smelled fresh and new.

"Do you wish to be alone?" he asked.

"Nay, my sorrow is no better when I am alone." She looked out across the water without really seeing it. "Will Sharla make do?"

"Aye, two MacDuffs already tried to claim her and she kicked one in the shins."

Jenae smiled. "At least Kristin will never know Sharla was her sister…or that Gordon was her uncle."

"True, she would not have liked knowing that at all."

"Yet she would have been thrilled to know Sile was her true aunt. What will become of Samuel now?"

"Father will see that he is well, we all will."

"Good. I think to take him a pie tomorrow."

"Will I be allowed to ride with you?"

Jenae ignored his comment. "Kristin loved you, she told me so."

"Aye, but perhaps not in the way you think. "Twas a trick to get her home."

"Nay, Tavan, she truly loved you."

He cast his gaze downward. There was a time when he wondered if she did, but that seemed ages ago. "I see."

"You did not love her?"

"I loved her, but not the way I love you."

She glanced at him and then quickly looked away. She picked up a yellow leaf, toyed with it a moment, shielded her eyes from the sun and looked up at the fall colors in the trees.

"Jenae, what is it?"

"I cannot. 'Tis too much at once."

At length, he stood up, started to leave and then turned back. "If I know my Mother, she has already told everyone that Kristin and I were not truly betrothed." He could think of nothing else to say. What could he say now that he had declared his love for her? All he could do now was wait -- wait for her to get beyond her sorrow and most of all, wait for her to forgive him.

*

Two weeks passed and then a third. Each morning, Tavan watched Jenae go to the graveyard, lay a flower on each of the two graves, and then ride off toward the gardens where she spent her days. He thought about going after her, but his mother advised him not to.

"Think how she must feel, son," Mackinzie said, sitting near him on the stonewall. "She knows Kristin loved you and had she survived, all would be fair if you chose Jenae. But Kristin is dead and having your love now is not fair to Kristin. Someday, Jenae will come to know Kristin would want both of you to be happy. She just does not know it yet, and there is nothing you or anyone can say to hurry her. Just wait, she will come to you when she is ready."

*

If Tavan was anxious, Sawney was beside himself. Each night he practically hung out of the upstairs window, hoping to see Jenae walk into the courtyard and join the other unmarried women. Each night, he was sorely disappointed. Jenae and Colina occasionally talked, but when he asked Colina if Jenae would marry Tavan, she simply shrugged.

Nevertheless, there was something very interesting going on. Samuel had taken to coming to the village each afternoon to take Sile riding. Her hips still pained her, so Samuel took her on his horse and didn't seem to mind holding her in his lap. He didn't seem to mind it at all.

Tavan couldn't sit still long enough to carve, although he tried often enough. His brothers attempted to keep him occupied, his sister-in-laws got him to play with the children, saying he needed the practice, but even that did not keep him from watching for Jenae.

Then it happened.

Sawney had had enough. He pushed his evening bowl aside, marched out the door and went to find Jenae. Everyone rushed out behind him and waited in the courtyard to see what he was up to. A few minutes later, he had Jenae by the hand. He took her to Tavan, put her hand in his son's and said, "I command you to walk. Walk I say, and do not come back until you are betrothed!"

Instead, Tavan took a smiling Jenae in his arms and kissed her…until she finally put her arms around his neck and kissed him back.

"Tis about time!" Sawney said, and then he put an arm around his daughter. "Now, Colina, I expect…"

-The end-

Coming Soon – Book 3 in the Viking series.

MORE MARTI TALBOTT BOOKS

Marti Talbott's Highlander Series: books 1 – 5 are short stories that follow the MacGreagor clan through two generations. They are followed by:

Betrothed, Book 6

The Golden Sword, Book 7

Abducted, Book 8

A Time of Madness, Book 9

Triplets, Book 10

Secrets, Book 11

Choices, Book 12

Ill-Fated Love Book 13

The Other Side of the River, Book 14

The Viking Series:

The Viking, Book 1 explains how the clan came into being.

The Viking's Daughter, Book 2

Book 3 is coming soon.

Marblestone Mansion (Scandalous Duchess Series) follows the MacGreagor clan into Colorado's early 20th century. There are currently 10 books in this series.

The Jackie Harlan Mysteries

Seattle Quake 9.2, Book 1

Missing Heiress, Book 2

Greed and a Mistress, Book 3

The Carson Series

The Promise, Book 1

Broken Pledge, Book 2

Talk to Marti on Facebook at:

https://www.facebook.com/marti.talbott

Sign up to be notified when new books are published at:

http://www.martitalbott.com

CPSIA information can be obtained at www.ICGtesting.com
Printed in the USA
BVOW05s1844080615

403701BV00002B/137/P